TREASURE HUNTERS

HUNTERS

DANGER DOWN THE NILE

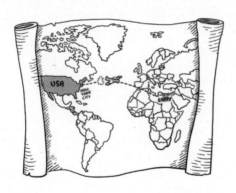

TREASURE HUNTERS

DANGER DOWN THE NILE

BY **JAMES PATTERSON**

AND CHRIS GRABENSTEIN

ILLUSTRATED BY
JULIANA NEUFELD

Published by Young Arrow, 2014

2 4 6 8 10 9 7 5 3 1

First published in Great Britain in 2014 by
Young Arrow
Random House, 20 Vauxhall Bridge Road,
London SW1V 2SA

www.randomhouse.co.uk

Addresses for companies within The Random House Group Limited can
be found at: www.randomhouse.co.uk/offices.htm

The Random House Group Limited Reg. No. 954009

A CIP catalogue record for this book
is available from the British Library

Hardback ISBN 9780099567639
Trade paperback ISBN 9780099567646

The Random House Group Limited supports the Forest Stewardship
Council® (FSC®), the leading international forest-certification
organisation. Our books carrying the FSC label are printed on
FSC®-certified paper. FSC is the only forest-certification scheme
supported by the leading environmental organisations, including
Greenpeace. Our paper procurement policy can be found at:
www.randomhouse.co.uk/environment

Printed and bound in Great Britain by Clays Ltd, St Ives plc

A QUICK NOTE FROM BICKFORD KIDD

First off, nobody calls me Bickford except my twin sister, Rebecca, and even then, only when she's really mad at me.

Second, you should know that I, Bick Kidd, will be the one telling you this story, while my sister Beck will be doing the drawings.

Like the one over on the next page.

(Beck just said I have to tell you not to believe everything I write, either. Especially if it's about her. Like my snarky comment about her snarky comments. Fine. Now, can we get on with the story?)

Hold on tight.

This could be a wild ride.

Hey, with us Kidds, most rides are.

PROLOGUE

BOTTOMING OUT

1

*A*ll my life, we Kidds have lived on the sea. Then, one day, we almost died under it.

The four of us were crammed inside a two-person mini-sub (what the US Navy calls a DSV, or Deep Submergence Vehicle), our newest piece of high-tech treasure-hunting gear. We'd purchased it at an auction with the half-million-dollar reward we collected on our last adventure.

My big sister, Storm, was convinced we needed the submarine to help us in our continuing quest to bring home the two most important treasures in the world: our missing mom and dad.

US KIDDS CRAMMED IN THE DSV.

COZY.

SMALL SPACES

ONCE AGAIN, BICK FORGETS TO BATHE. AND BRUSH HIS TEETH. AND NOT EAT BEAN BURRITOS ON A DIVE DAY.

See, Storm doesn't dive, because the last time she climbed into a rubber scuba suit, some mean old geezer on a yacht called her a "shrink-wrapped whale." Obviously, that little comment wasn't his best idea, because the next time he went to take his fancy yacht for a spin, the fish-head-in-your-bedsheets smell was getting pretty bad. Nobody messes with Storm.

We still needed Storm's photographic memory if we wanted to go back to the pair of sunken Spanish galleons off the coast of Florida that

2

our father, the world-famous treasure hunter Dr. Thomas Kidd, had dubbed the Twins. That was why we were packed like sardines in the DSV.

Unfortunately, Mom and Dad weren't with us.

The ships' cargo holds were loaded down with treasure—enough to finance Kidd Family Treasure Hunters Inc. for as long as it took to figure out some way to help our parents, who—on top of being world-class treasure hunters—were neck-deep in dangerous CIA business.

So finding those ships was crazy important.

But Tommy had lost the treasure map that took us to the Twins the first time. Well, if we're being honest, he accidentally used it as a napkin for a greasy slice of pizza, then crumpled it up and tossed it into a trash barrel. A trash barrel he and one of his assorted girlfriends used later for a beach bonfire.

So it was pretty much gone for good.

"This sub is awesome!" said Tommy, who's seventeen and the closest thing we have to adult supervision. "The four of us can dive as a family without messing up our hair."

"Or breathing," added Beck, who was squished up against a porthole.

"Change your heading to two hundred and sixty-three degrees, Tommy," said Storm, navigating from memory. "The sunken vessels will be dead ahead."

"Aye, aye," said Tommy.

But when he nudged the control stick forward, the ship didn't budge.

We kept drifting downward.

Sinking deeper.

And deeper.

"Um, how far down can this thing go without popping a gasket?" I asked.

"Forty-five hundred meters," said Storm. "That's fourteen thousand seven hundred and sixty-four feet, for those of you who skipped the math chapter on metric conversions."

"Maybe we should go back up to *The Lost*," suggested Beck. "And, oh, I don't know—read the operating manual?"

"Yeah," said Tommy. "That'd be a good idea. Make all preparations for surfacing. Secure the ventilation. Shut bulkhead flappers."

Yep. Tommy sure sounded like a real, live submarine commander.

Too bad we kept sinking.

"Uh, those controls aren't working, either," Tommy finally said after nothing he flipped or poked worked.

"So, basically," I said, "all we can do is keep going down? To the bottom of the sea?"

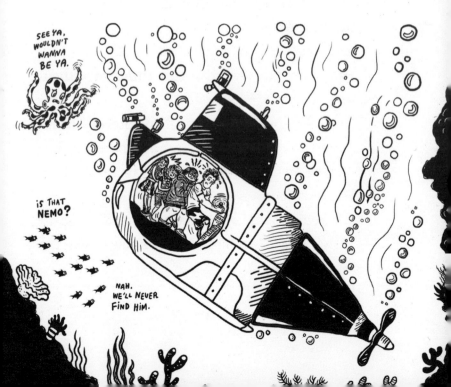

Tommy nodded. "Basically."

That was when our engines cut out.

"We've lost power," Storm reported matter-of-factly. "If you have a favorite prayer, now would be a good time to start reciting it."

Remember how Tommy said that thing about the sub making it easier for us to dive as a family?

Well, it looked like it might help us *die* as a family, too!

We kept drifting down.

"Good-bye, cruel world," said Storm, who's sort of known for blurting out whatever is on her mind whenever it happens to be there. "Tell Neptune to stick his forked trident in our butts, because we're done. It's all over but the crying—except, of course, I refuse to do it."

"Hey, hang on," said Tommy. "We're the Kidds. We live for dangerous adventures like this. Death-defying explorations are the Krazy Glue that holds us together. Sure, sometimes we get down, but we always get back up. And we're never, *ever* defeated!"

Yes, my big brother was being a rock. Or a blockhead.

I mean, seriously, we were in deep trouble—like almost-all-the-way-down-to-the-bottom-of-the-ocean deep.

"You know, Tommy," said Beck, "you kind of remind me of Dad. Bucking us up like that. It's sweet."

Tommy gave her his dimpled grin. "Thanks, Beck."

"It's also kind of tragic," added Storm. "Especially given the timing. However, since we still have a few hours of oxygen left, we have plenty of time to contemplate our coming deaths while ruminating on the things in life that we'll miss the most. For me, it's a toss-up: Mallomars or Krispy Kremes?"

"Oh, tough call, Storm," Beck said. "I have to give it to the classic Mallomar, though."

"What about Mom and Dad?" I said. "That's what I'll miss."

Pirates in Cyprus had kidnapped our mother. Our father had been missing ever since we battled a terrifying tropical storm off the coast of the Cayman Islands. I had, with our uncle Timothy's help, sent a fake e-mail from "Dad" to "his" kids, but that hadn't completely convinced everyone he was still alive.

Storm set her jaw. "Dad is already dead, Bick. You need to accept that fact and move on."

"Where's he going to move to?" said Beck. "We're squished inside here like Pokémon trapped inside a Poké Ball!"

"Storm's right," said Tommy with a sigh. "Dad's waiting for us, down below in Davy Jones's locker."

"Okay—who is this guy Davy with the locker, anyway?" asked Beck. "Some gym class reject?"

"Look, you guys," I shouted, probably wasting way more oxygen than I should have. "Dad is *not* dead! Just because he disappeared off the deck of *The Lost* in the middle of a hurricane-sized storm doesn't mean anything."

Storm stared at me. "Except that he's dead."

She slumped her shoulders and then proved that she's not always as cold as she pretends to be: She just collapsed to the floor in despair.

She landed so hard that the whole vessel shook.

And the submarine started sinking even faster.

Okay, by now you've figured out that we didn't actually die at the bottom of the sea. I mean, this is just the prologue. Narrators never die in the prologue.

(But Beck says it's okay if I do. She'll take over for me. Gee, thanks, sis.)

So how did we survive?

Well, when we hit the ocean floor, it was like somebody kicking an ornery vending machine.

Suddenly all the lights on the control panels flickered to life. The stone-cold-dead engines fired up.

"Excellent. We bottomed out hard enough to jump-start all the systems," explained Storm.

Tommy pulled back on the control stick and we headed to the surface.

"Why don't we come back for the treasure the old-fashioned way?" I suggested. "Let's put on our scuba gear and dive for it."

"Fine," said Beck. "It'll beat being stuck inside this bobbing barrel with your barracuda breath!"

We all laughed.

I don't think any of us had been happier since maybe the last Christmas we spent with Mom and Dad together in Pago Pago.

That is, until we sliced through the foamy breakers at the surface.

Because another—very large, very menacing—submarine was up there waiting for us.

I t was Nathan Collier's submarine.

The same Nathan Collier who was Mom and Dad's number one nemesis: the smiling sleazeball with his own cable TV show on the Underwater Weirdo Channel. The skeevoid was always trying to steal our parents' glory and claim credit for their discoveries when, in truth, he was the worst treasure hunter to ever sail the seven seas (he thought there were only five).

"Ahoy, Kidds!" Collier shouted through a bullhorn from the deck of his submarine, where he stood surrounded by heavily armed thugs.

Collier, who is about as tall as I am, even though technically he's an adult, was decked out in his official explorer costume: khaki pants, khaki shirt, and a faded leather bomber jacket. His hair was plastered into place, with one spit curl dangling over his left eyebrow. His cheesy smile was cheesier than a cheeseball from Cheesylvania.

"You children will never believe what I just discovered down below. Two of the Spanish galleons from Córdoba's Lost Fleet of 1605. My sonar readings confirm that the twin ships are *loaded* with treasure!"

The Twins.

What Dad used to call our "Secret College Fund."

"Those shipwrecks are ours!" hollered Tommy.

"Oh, really? Did you or your parents file the paperwork necessary to authenticate your claim?"

Tommy started mumbling to himself. "No. It was our *secret* treasure stash....You don't do paperwork for secrets...."

"Really?" said Collier. "Because I just did!" He waved a sheet of paper in the air. "Gina helped me."

"Hiya, Tommy!"

A redhead in a polka-dot bikini wiggled up out of Collier's submarine hatch. Of course it would have to be one of Tommy's many ex-girlfriends.

"Nathan's going to give me some of the Spanish queen's emeralds for helping him track you guys," Gina gushed. "So thank you, Tommy, for giving me your cell number!"

"You know, Thomas," Collier teased, "you really should deactivate the GPS chip in your smartphone from time to time. Especially if you don't want all your brokenhearted girlfriends to know exactly where they can find you at all times."

Tommy looked at us with sad eyes. "Sorry, you guys."

"That's okay," I said. "Let Collier have the gold."

"Yeah," said Beck. "Let him take all the jewelry, too."

"And the priceless religious artifacts," added Storm.

"Not to mention the silver," said Beck. "Silver's almost as good as gold...."

"It doesn't matter," I said. "We're the Kidds! Nothing's worth more than that!"

"Actually," said Storm, "the total monetary value of all the minerals in our bodies is four dollars and fifty cents. Each."

"Well," I said, trying my best to boost morale, "I still say family is more valuable than gold. Even if we lose all that treasure, we still have one another!"

"And now," announced Collier, "I must ask you four children to climb back into your tiny toy boat so I can torpedo it and tell the world how your reckless treasure-hunting antics led to your untimely deaths."

Okay. So maybe we wouldn't have one another much longer, either.

Beck balled up her fist and shook it at Collier. "You'll pay for this, you…you…you…"

I helped her out. "…Scurvy, scum-sucking blowhole of a bilge pump!"

"Ooh. Nice one, Bick."

"Thanks. You do the pictures, I do the words."

"Forget the boat!" shouted Collier. "You nasty, detestable Kidds have been a barnacle on my butt long enough."

He turned to his troops to give them the command to open fire on us.

But he hesitated when a fleet of stealthy speedboats appeared on the horizon.

"Put down your weapons!" ordered an amplified voice over the lead boat's loudspeaker system. "We have you surrounded, Collier!"

It was our sort-of uncle Timothy, the strange and mysterious superspy who, supposedly, managed

Mom and Dad's top-secret CIA missions and always seemed to know exactly when and where to show up.

We were saved!

Or were we?

STAND DOWN! WE'RE FROM THE CIA!

HOWEVER, WE'RE SUPERSECRET SPIES, SO FORGET I JUST SAID THAT.

PART 1

THE HUNT FOR OUR NEXT TREASURE HUNT

CHAPTER 1

Even though fake Uncle Timothy isn't really a member of our family, guess where he dragged us?

To Family Court. In New York City.

"Your Honor," said Uncle Timothy, who took off his mirrored sunglasses only because the bailiff told him he had to, "allow me to present Exhibits A, B, C, and D." Uncle Timothy was acting as an attorney because I guess when you get high enough in the CIA they let you do whatever you want.

He handed the judge four very official-looking documents.

"As you can see by these affidavits, the late Dr. Thomas Kidd designated me to be the legal guardian for his four children in the event of his untimely death."

I stood up. "Objection, Your Honor!"

"Who are you?"

"Bickford Kidd. Our dad isn't dead!"

The judge banged his gavel. "Sit down!"

I did as I was told.

The judge shuffled through the guardianship papers, then peered over the rims of his reading glasses. "Where is their mother?"

"Detained, Your Honor," said Uncle Timothy. "High-level negotiations are currently under way with her kidnappers in Cyprus. However, it seems her days are numbered."

"Excuse me?"

"The negotiations aren't going very well, sir. Mrs. Kidd may be dead. Soon."

All four of us gasped when fake Uncle Timothy said that—even Storm, who's never big on public displays of emotion.

This was the worst news we'd heard in weeks. Maybe even in our lives.

Mom should've been set free by now. We'd found the Grecian urn her kidnappers had demanded for her ransom. It'd been shipped over to Cyprus. We'd done everything we were supposed to do and still the bad guys wouldn't let Mom go?

"Your Honor," said pretend Uncle Timothy, "I hereby petition the court to grant me sole conservatorship over all the Kidd family assets so I might manage their various bank and investment accounts, the assorted safe-deposit boxes scattered around town, and, of course, the family's sailing vessel, *The Lost*."

"In such extraordinary circumstances—" the judge began.

"Hang on just one second, Your Judiciousness!" Beck interrupted. "You can't just give our assets over to someone just because they come to court with fancy papers! That's not fair!"

"Yeah," I joined in. "Plus Dad's not dead! He was only washed overboard in a massive storm."

"Your Honor, young Bickford and Rebecca here have just provided more evidence that the Kidd children are still just that: children. According to the papers signed by their deceased father, my petition is legally the only course of action."

"I tend to agree," said the judge, who seemed like he was just waking up from a daydream. "Having carefully reviewed the available evidence, I've decided that your petition is granted."

"*Carefully?!?*" Storm bellowed indignantly.

"Define *carefully!*" Beck yelled, jumping out of her chair.

"But—but—" I stammered. Tommy and I were still in shock. This guy wasn't giving us the time of day.

The judge ignored us and banged his gavel again. "I hereby hand over control of the Kidd family assets to Mr. Timothy Quinn."

All of us Kidds started protesting incoherently at the judge.

"*Quiet!!!*" all the adults shouted over the chaos, and for some reason, we all shut up, like we were goody-two-shoes kids or something.

Turning to address Uncle Timothy, the judge asked, "And what about the children? Will they be living with you?"

"No, Your Honor. As much as I would enjoy that"—Uncle Timothy was *soooo* lying—"I think it best that I fulfill their father's fondest wish and enroll all four children in New York City's prestigious Chumley Prep, the same boarding school where Dr. Thomas Kidd, himself, once matriculated."

Wait a second. School?

We'd never been to school a day in our lives.

Man, could this get any worse?

CHAPTER 2

All our lives, Tommy, Storm, Beck, and I have been homeschooled by Mom and Dad aboard *The Lost*.

And even though both of them had been seriously missing for a while, the four of us still totally respected and followed their three-hours-a-day study rule.

Sending us to a real school—one with desks and interactive whiteboards and cafeteria food—would have to be considered cruel and unusual punishment.

Except, of course, by our judge.

"Let me state, for the record," the judge proclaimed, "that I am appalled that these four children have been attempting to take charge of their lives without any adult supervision. Children are incapable of responsible behavior. Therefore, I hereby grant Timothy Quinn full and complete control over all their financial affairs."

That was when Storm stood up and marched over to the judge. She was furious.

"May a condemned child speak prior to her execution?" Storm demanded.

"Which one are you?" asked the judge.

"That's Stephanie," said bogus Uncle Timothy.

Storm's eyes became darker than thunderclouds bristling with lightning bolts when Uncle Timothy insulted her like that. Yep. That was why Mom and Dad nicknamed Stephanie "Storm."

"If it pleases the court, you, sir, are not worthy to be a judge of other people. You have no compassion and, actually, you don't seem all that smart, either. I rest my case."

Storm sat down.

The judge banged his gavel again.

"You need to learn a lesson, young lady," he decreed. "You all do! Therefore, the Kidd family sailing vessel known as *The Lost* and all its contents shall be sold at auction, posthaste, with any and all proceeds from that sale being applied to the tuition, books, and boarding fees for Chumley Prep's four newest students."

And that was that.

We were going to school. *The Lost* was going to the highest bidder.

Justice wasn't just blind that day. It was totally unfair, too.

CHAPTER 3

Saturday morning we headed down to the docks to say good-bye to the only home we had ever known.

The Lost.

The ship that sailed us around the world. Twice. The boat that was a huge part of our family's most exciting adventures.

Watching the vultures descend on her decks and strip her of everything she had—even the stuff hidden inside some of the supercool, secret compartments Dad had built into the masts, hull, and deck—was too much. Beck and I erupted into what our parents used to call a Twin Tirade.

Of course, the first time Mom and Dad called our screamfests a "tirade," I had no idea what the word meant. So Mom (our onboard ELA instructor) made me look it up: "*ti·rade*: a long, angry speech of criticism or accusation."

Basically, there's lots of shouting and name-calling (the names I come up with are way better than Beck's). But our Twin Tirades are never really "long." In fact, they usually last about sixty seconds and then we're done. They're sort of like the big finale in a Fourth of July fireworks show. Lots of explosions, with sparks flying off in every direction and then—*poof!*—a minute later, it's over. There's nothing left but a few puffs of smoke and a sky full of stars.

Twin Tirade No. 442 started when I said watching scavengers strip *The Lost* was the worst thing to ever happen to us.

"Oh, really?" said Beck. "What about the night Dad died?"

"He didn't die."

"Yes, he did."

"No, he did not."

"Um, excuse me, Bickford, but if Dad's so alive, why hasn't he sent us some kind of message?"

"Uh, he already did, Rebecca. Remember?"

"Oh, you mean that bogus e-mail you sent us in North Carolina?"

"Dad sent that."

"No, Bickford, *you* did."

"Says who?"

"Me, you dummy!"

(See what I mean about Beck's name-calling abilities?)

"So what if you say I wrote it?" I snapped back. "You're nothing but a demented ink dribbler!"

"I'm also your twin sister, Bickford. That means we're totally connected. So I know every time you even think about doing something sneaky."

"Really? You do?"

"Totally."

"Wow. So you knew I wrote that e-mail?"

"You did?"

"What? Yeah."

"Ha! I knew it."

"But you didn't before?"

"Nope."

"That was actually sneaky, Beck."

"So? Didn't you know I was going to trick you?"

"No, not really."

"Huh. Me neither. Guess we're not as totally connected as I thought."

"Yeah, I guess not."

And then we were done.

Of course, Beck now knew that I had faked the e-mail from Dad and that I had absolutely no proof our father was still alive.

Until one of the boat scavengers ripped open some deck planks up in the bow.

CHAPTER 4

"What'd you find, Rizzo?" asked the ship hunter's partner.

"Another one of them secret compartments."

"Anything good inside?"

"Nah. Nothin' but a stupid yellow rain slicker like that guy on the fish sticks box wears."

"That's my dad's!" I shouted. Then I grabbed a rope line and swung aboard *The Lost*, pirate-style. "He was wearing it the night of the storm! It's not for sale."

The scruffy-looking man named Rizzo nodded like he understood. "Sentimental value, huh, kid?"

"Yeah."

And he handed me the yellow rain slicker.

"Hang on to it, kid. Maybe one day you'll be big enough to wear it."

"Thanks." I bundled the jacket up tight and clutched it against my chest.

On the night of the big storm, when waves the size of rolling mountains nearly swamped *The Lost*, my father had been wearing this very same slicker.

So I had to ask myself: *Why did he take it off and hide it in a secret compartment none of us even knew existed?*

It had to be some kind of a message from Dad!

Maybe he didn't get washed overboard. Maybe he really did get rescued off the deck of our ship by a CIA helicopter, which was the story I'd made up for that fake e-mail Beck had just busted me on.

I searched through the rubbery jacket's pockets, hoping to find a quickly scribbled note.

Nothing.

I turned it inside out.

Nothing. Just a label in the collar: MADE IN CHINA.

36

The slicker was so old a couple of the letters in the word *made* had been worn down and practically rubbed away.

But that was it. There was no message except the obvious one: If, on the night of the terrible storm, Dad had taken the time to stow his rain gear in a safe hiding place, he must've known he'd be coming back to wear it again.

I smiled for the first time in days.

Because the rain slicker was the first solid clue any of us had found that Dad was still alive!

CHAPTER 5

So did losing *The Lost* mark the end of the Kidds? Are you kidding?!?

We laugh in the face of defeat. *Ha, ha, ha!*

And, sometimes, defeat laughs at us, too. Like on our first day of school at Chumley Prep.

Hee, hee, hee.

That was defeat laughing its butt off because Tommy and I had to wear these dorky blazers with Chumley Prep patches stitched over the breast pocket. We also had to wear white shirts and striped ties. Worst of all, we had to wear neatly pressed pants.

Hey, a lot of the time on board *The Lost*, we'd run around in swim trunks or shorts. Pants itch. Especially gray woolen slacks. I don't know why sheep don't scratch their legs all day long.

As bad as Chumley Prep was for Tommy and me, it was even worse for Beck and Storm. They had to wear plaid skirts and blouses with frilly collars. They were supposed to wear plaid bows in their hair, too, but the lady in charge of the girls' dormitory lost that particular stare-down.

Long story short, school was miserable.

See, we Kidds are a lot like the wild things in that book by Maurice Sendak, where the wild things roar their terrible roars and gnash their terrible teeth. Beck even has wild thing hair. I think I got the terrible teeth.

Putting the Kidd kids in a school with structure and attendance and having to raise your hand every time you needed to go to the bathroom was a lot like taking those wild things and locking them up in zoo cages. We lived for action and adventure, not rule following and test taking. And trust me, you can learn a lot more about the colonization of the New World by swimming around inside a sunken Spanish galleon salvaging conquistador helmets than you'll ever learn from a world history book.

I'm sure school is fine for a lot of kids, but not The Kidds. It was crushing our spirits, forcing us to spend time with teachers who were smart but not half as much fun as our mother and father.

And then there was Mrs. McSorley, an ancient librarian who kept bugging Tommy about an overdue library book he swore he never checked out.

"We've only been here a week," he told her when she confronted him outside the headmaster's office. "I don't even know where the library is yet."

"Your name is Thomas Kidd, is it not?"

"Totally."

"And did you not, on October the thirteenth, nineteen hundred and eighty-two, check out *The World's Greatest Treasures* by Sir Walter Quinn?"

"Um, don't think so. See, I wasn't even born in 1982."

"A likely story. Bring that book back to the library, Mr. Kidd. Or I will mention this matter to the headmaster!"

After Mrs. McSorley stomped away, Tommy and I realized something: Dad, the original Thomas Kidd, was probably the one who had checked out that book!

"He must have taken it out way back when he was a student here," I said.

Tommy just nodded and got a far-off look in his eye—I mean more far-off than usual. (Mom and Dad called Tommy "Tailspin" because he always looks a little confused.)

"Huh," he said. Then he said it again. "Huh."

"What?"

"Well, the book is called *The World's Greatest Treasures*. And when I was little, back before you and Beck were even born, Dad used to say, 'Tommy, if I ever found the world's greatest treasures, I'd hide them where no one would dare look—inside the boys' room of my old prep school.'"

"You think he meant the book?"

"Only one way to find out. We need to round up Beck and Storm. It's time for an indoor treasure hunt!"

CHAPTER 6

Meals at Chumley Prep were served in a giant dining hall that looked a lot like the one in the Harry Potter movies, minus all the magic.

And we still had to wear our stupid school uniforms.

But dinner was the one time every day when all four of us were able to be together in semi-privacy. None of the other boarding students wanted to sit with us—not after Beck and I had Twin Tirade No. 445 about which fork you're supposed to use first and who gets which bread plate.

"You guys up for a treasure hunt?" Tommy whispered to Storm and Beck as we all pushed

NOBODY WANTS TO SIT NEAR US. MUST BE BICK'S REPULSIVE PERSONALITY.

around our dull mashed potatoes, peas, and meat-loaf.

"What's the treasure?" asked Beck.

"A book!" I blurted.

"Oh, wow. A book. Awesome." That was Beck being sarcastic.

"It's one we think Dad checked out when he was a student here," I explained in a hushed voice. "*The World's Greatest Treasures* by Sir Walter

Quinn. He used to tell Tommy about it all the time."

Storm nodded. "Like if he ever found 'the world's greatest treasures,' he'd hide them where nobody would dare look?"

"Chyah!" said Tommy. "Inside the boys' room of—"

"His old prep school," said Storm. "He told me the same thing."

"That's this place," said Beck, finally catching on. "It could be a clue!"

And so, that night, a little after midnight, the four of us snuck out of our dorm rooms and met up in the central hall underneath the dark oil portrait of Cornelius Chumley, the dead guy with bushy sideburns the school was named after.

"There's a boys' room on every floor," whispered Tommy as I passed around floor plans of the school. I had marked each of our target bathrooms with a big red X.

Storm raised her hand.

"Yeah?" said Tommy.

"Can Beck and I go into the boys' bathroom? Isn't that both against the rules and supergross?"

OFF TO FIND THE LOST TREASURE OF THE TOILET BOWL!

"Don't worry," I said. "The teachers and janitors are all asleep or have gone home."

Storm stared at me blankly. "Worrying is what I do best, Bick."

"You and Beck can wait outside while Bick and I go in," said Tommy.

"No way," said Beck. "I've always wanted to see what's inside the boys' room. I mean, besides the filth and stench."

So the four of us quietly tiptoed up a staircase

47

to the fourth-floor bathrooms. Tommy, Beck, and I went in. Storm stood guard in the hall.

After a quick search of the sinks, urinals, towel dispensers, and toilet stalls, we found nothing. Well, nothing you could call a treasure, unless you have a thing for ancient limericks carved into wooden doors.

The same thing was true on the third floor.

But, on the second floor, we hit pay dirt.

CHAPTER 7

Believe it or not, the missing book was sealed inside a half-gallon-sized Ziploc plastic bag and jammed up behind the old-fashioned elevated toilet tank in the middle stall.

We took the treasure package into the hall, where Storm was.

"Open it up!" said Beck.

Tommy pried open the Ziploc seal. The book inside was a musty, wrinkled mess. Decades of toilet-tank moisture had taken their toll on the paper pages, even though they had been sealed in plastic. They were completely stuck together.

"I think we owe the school a new book," I said.

IT'S MORE LIKE A **BRICK** THAN A BOOK. ↓

"What's that?" asked Storm, pointing to a rusty, antique key attached to a narrow band of leather that was poking up behind the warped book's front cover.

"Looks like a bookmark," said Beck. "Or a really awkward key chain."

Tommy managed to pull the bookmark free of the water-damaged book's grip.

Chunky block letters had been hammered into the side of the faded leather strip to spell out an inspirational message: READING IS THE KEY TO ALL OF LIFE'S TREASURES.

"Sweet," said Tommy, passing it to Beck so she could look at it.

"Yeah," said Beck. "Dad probably bought it at a Hallmark store when he was feeling sentimental—or maybe just mental."

"Or," I said, taking the bookmark from Beck, "it could be a clue."

"To what?"

Suddenly all the lights in the hallway snapped on.

"To what you four should be doing instead of skulking around the school corridors in the middle of the night: Reading!"

It was the headmaster. And the librarian.

"Ah-hah!" said Mrs. McSorley, marching over to Tommy to snatch the book out of his hands. "I see you found my missing Quinn. The fine for overdue library books at this school is twenty cents per day. Therefore, Thomas Kidd, you owe me..."

She twiddled her fingers while she figured it out.

"Two thousand three hundred and thirty-six dollars."

"Um, we're kind of broke," said Tommy.

Now the librarian sniffed the moldy paper, then tried to pry the book open.

"This book has been damaged! You must purchase a replacement."

"Put it on our tab," cracked Beck.

"Oh, we will," said the headmaster. "And we'll send the bill directly to your legal guardian and financial custodian."

Uncle Timothy.

The slippery spook in the sunglasses who had all our money while we had nothing.

Except, of course, Dad's old leather bookmark, which I had tucked into the back pocket of my itchy woolen pants back when Mrs. McSorley was playing her air calculator.

is THE KEY
THE KEY?

CHAPTER 8

To prove how NOT defeated we were by all the bad stuff that'd been happening, that night, after the librarian took away Dad's hidden book, the four of us held a quick family meeting and decided that we needed to start planning our next *real* treasure hunt.

Not another indoor bathroom excursion. Something epic and exciting, full of high risk and big reward.

By the way, where do *you* think we should go next?

(And no, Beck, "math class" is not the kind of

answer I'm looking for here. "Far, far away" isn't helpful, either.)

Anyway, we were more or less focused on four big moneymakers. Yes, we love archaeology, but, thanks to fake Uncle Timothy, we had what they call a "cash flow" problem. We needed money, and we needed it fast, so we couldn't necessarily be as picky as we wanted to be with our next hunt. The plan had been to go straight for King Solomon's Mines, but it looked like we might have to cast a wider net.

Our top four choices were in or around Africa, based on some of the hunches that Mom and Dad used to talk about:

1. **King Solomon's Mines.** During wise King Solomon's long reign in the tenth century BC, the kingdom of the Hebrews was extremely wealthy. Trading expeditions would return to the capital city of Jerusalem with all sorts of exquisite stones (diamonds and rubies) from mines rumored to be somewhere in the middle of Africa!

I HOPE THEY HAVE A RUNAWAY MINE TRAIN LIKE AT DISNEY WORLD.

2. **Kruger's Hidden Millions.** We're not talking about Freddy Krueger. The legendary Kruger Millions is the treasure hidden by Stephanus Johannes Paulus Kruger, the guy with a lot of names who was state president of the South African Republic (Transvaal) and led the Boer Resistance against the British during the Second Boer War (1899–1902). Despite

its name, the war was very exciting. When Mr. Kruger fled the city of Pretoria, he took a ton of gold bullion with him. At today's prices, it'd be worth $243 million. No one has ever found it.

3. **The Ming Dynasty's Artifacts from Zheng He's Treasure Fleet.** In the early fifteenth century, the Ming Dynasty in China sent out a fleet of mammoth treasure junks (each boat was four hundred feet long) that made seven epic voyages from Nanjing to India, Arabia,

CHRISTOPHER COLUMBUS'S SHIP WOULD HAVE BEEN A LIFEBOAT ON A CHINESE TREASURE SHIP! THOSE THINGS WERE **HUGE** AND LOADED WITH TREASURE.

and East Africa. Once, off the coast of Kenya, pirates attacked several of the humongous Chinese treasure ships. Zheng He fought back and won—but not before one of his supersized jumbo junks, loaded down with treasure and tribute, ended up as jumbled junk at the bottom of the sea.

4. **La Buse's (The Buzzard's) Abandoned Pirate Treasure.** Olivier Levasseur (1688–1730) was a pirate everybody called *La Buse* (*The Buzzard*) because of the fast and furious (not to mention ruthless) way he attacked his enemies. He also had a gnarly scar across one of his eyes. Very buzzard-ish. The Buzzard pillaged and plundered off the coast of Madagascar and East Africa for decades. When he

MEET *The* BUZZARD.

REMINDS ME OF BICK FIRST THING IN THE MORNING.

was finally captured and sentenced to death, he stood on the hangman's scaffold with a necklace dangling around his neck. On it was a square filled with a cryptogram—seventeen lines of secret code. He ripped the thing off and flung it to the crowd, saying, "Find my treasure, ye who may understand it." Treasure hunters have been searching for his hidden booty ever since.

Whatever treasure we decided to track down, we knew we were definitely going to Africa because we needed to swing by Egypt first.

Why?

Because that was where our mother told us to go.

CHAPTER 9

This is how incredibly amazing our mom is: Even though she was still being held by kidnappers over in Cyprus, she found a way to smuggle some secret instructions to us.

How'd she do it?

Through Dr. Louis Lewis, professor of Ancient Near Eastern Art and Archaeology at Columbia University in New York City. He had helped us on our last adventure. Now he found us at Chumley Prep to tell us he had actually seen Mom over in Cyprus and had brought back "her top-secret message"!

Dr. Lewis agreed to meet us first thing Saturday morning in Central Park. We headed for the benches circling Cleopatra's Needle, a four-sided obelisk inscribed with Egyptian hieroglyphics that's on a knoll right behind the Metropolitan Museum of Art.

Professor Lewis, decked out in his rumpled tweed sports coat with patches sewn on the elbows, was feeding pigeons the crumbs left over from his bag of buttered bagels.

"Ah! The Kidd brood. Thank you for meeting me here. It's lovely to see you again."

"How's our mother?" blurted Storm, who usually skips the chitchat and cuts to the chase.

"Holding up as well as can be expected given that she is currently at the mercy of that merciless band of brigands."

"But she's okay?" I asked. "She's not dead or anything?"

"Oh, no. Far from it. In fact, she's still giving her captors plenty of what she calls ''tude.'"

"So you were with her in Cyprus?" said Tommy, who's usually a page or two behind everybody else—even if it's a comic book.

"Indeed, I was. Her kidnappers requested my

presence once they took possession of the Grecian urn, which you children so expertly tracked down. I wholeheartedly supported your mother's authentication of the priceless artifact."

"And they still wouldn't let her go?"

Dr. Lewis shook his head. "I'm afraid not. However, in exchange for my services, they did allow me to depart Cyprus with this."

He held up a slender thumb drive.

"What's on it?" I asked.

"A video message. From your mother."

CHAPTER 10

After we hurried back to Chumley Prep, Storm grabbed her laptop and we found a quiet room where we could watch the mysterious video in private.

It wasn't very long, but it was extremely powerful and moving.

Because it was of our mom talking directly to the camera.

"Hello, kids."

Mom smiled like she did every time she called us "kids" since, you know, we're "Kidds."

"I can't tell you how much I miss you guys and your dad. I heard about the trouble on the boat. Tommy? You're in charge until your father and I return. You've always been brave. We know you won't let us down."

"I won't, Mom. I promise." Tommy raised his right hand like he was making a solemn oath.

"But, Tommy? Always listen to Storm—my beautiful, brainy daughter. She's smarter than anyone I have ever met. And she will never forget the most important thing in the world—how much she loves her family."

Tommy draped his arm around Storm. She gave him a sideways look but let his arm stay on her shoulder anyhow.

"And both of you—watch out for your little brother and sister. My terrific twins! Oh, Beck, how I miss your drawings. By now, you're probably better than Picasso."

THE **KiDD** FAMiLY
Picasso STYLE →

BECK KIDD

"Close," muttered Beck.

"And Bick—before I fall asleep every night, I tell myself one of your stories. They make me smile, no matter how bad my day's been. You should write them down so everybody can enjoy them as much as I do."

There was a slight pause. Mom's eyes darted to the right.

"Oh-kay. My, um, *hosts* just said I need to

speed this up a little. So pay very close attention to what I'm about to say. As you can see, I've lost all track of time. But please go visit my aunt Bela Kilgore. She's in Cairo. And remember, kids— winter, spring, summer, and fall, my aunt Bela loves Julius Caesar and the number thirteen most of all. Also, if you ever meet a man in an eye patch with a pencil-thin mustache who happens to be wearing a French Foreign Legion hat, run away! Tell Aunt Bela to run away, too. His name is Guy Dubonnet Merck and—"

A shadowy figure stepped in front of the camera lens and grunted something like, "Enough. Turn it off."

The screen went black.

So did my brain.

Because I was totally confused.

CHAPTER 11

What was all that mumbo jumbo about Aunt Bela, Julius Caesar, the number thirteen, and a nasty man named Guy in a French Foreign Legion hat with an eye patch?

"Okay," said Beck. "That was, like, totally random."

"No, it wasn't," I said, not really in the mood for another Twin Tirade. "What if *Aunt* Bela is the same as *Uncle* Timothy?"

"You mean she's a guy?" said Tommy.

"No," said Beck. "Guy's the one with the funny hat who's missing an eyeball."

"That's not what I meant," I said. "*Uncle* Timothy is Mom and Dad's CIA handler, right?

Well, what if *Aunt* Bela is another CIA boss?"

"Oh," said Tommy. "Cool. Way to figure junk out, Bick."

"Thanks. And, if Bela Kilgore is CIA, too, she might know what we need to do to rescue Mom."

Storm shrugged. "Maybe. By the way, Mom also lost her watch."

"Huh?" said Tommy.

"When Mom said she'd 'lost all track of time,' did you notice her right wrist?"

We all shook our heads.

"She wasn't wearing her Breitling Superocean Heritage Chronograph."

"Huh?" said Tommy. Again.

"Her dive watch. With a suggested retail price of close to seven thousand dollars, it was likely stolen by the kidnappers."

With her photographic memory, Storm not

MOM'S WRIST.
NOTE THE WATCH TAN LINE!

only notices every tiny detail (like Mom's missing watch), but she can recite catalog information about it, too.

"We need to be in Egypt," mumbled Tommy.

Yes, for the first time since forever, we were all about to disobey one of our parents' direct orders to study hard.

None of us were very focused on our schoolwork.

In fact, we were all about to become prep school dropouts.

CHAPTER 12

That night at zero-dark-thirty (that's spy lingo for thirty minutes after midnight), the four of us met underneath the portrait of Cornelius Chumley down in the prep school's central hall.

HOW TO EARN A YEAR'S WORTH OF UNEXCUSED ABSENCES IN ONE NIGHT.

Each of us had packed a quick Go Bag. I'd stuffed some clothes, my journal, a book I'd been reading, half a Snickers bar, a dollar fifty in loose change, Mom's thumb drive, and Dad's old rain slicker into my backpack. Beck packed Dad's leather bookmark, as well as her pen set and sketchpad. Tommy probably loaded his whole duffel with hair products and Axe body spray.

All of us were dressed in our best stealthy commando outfits: all black-on-black clothes with rubber-soled running shoes. Beck had even dabbed some black India ink under her eyes, so she sort of looked like a football player.

"You guys ready to do this thing?" Tommy asked in a whisper.

"I was born ready," said Beck.

"Me too," I added.

"I know," Beck shot back. "I was there."

"True," I said. "But I was there first."

"By two minutes."

"First is first, Beck."

"Which is why you're a first-class freakazoid, Bick."

We were about to erupt into Twin Tirade
No. 461 when Storm raised her hand.

"Yeah?" said Tommy, our fearless leader.

"Where exactly are we escaping to?" Storm
asked.

"Cairo. Egypt."

Storm arched an eyebrow. "And which sub-
way train do you recommend we take to get
there?"

"Look," said Tommy. "We'll figure out all the
details later. Right now—"

The lights snapped on overhead.

"Where do you children think you're going
at this hour?"

It was Mr. Norby, the night watchman.

Tommy thought fast. "Um, out?"

"We need pencils," I added. "For, uh, school
tomorrow!"

And then we started running.

Good thing Mr. Norby is old—like, in his
nineties. He wheezes a lot and has hair growing
inside his ears.

We darted past him.

"Stop!" he shouted. "No running! Running is against the rules...."

By the time we hit the front doors, Mr. Norby was winded.

We dashed down Chumley Prep's front steps and reached the New York City sidewalk. The fresh night air smelled like freedom!

But there was a black town car parked at the curb. The driver's window scrolled down.

An Asian man was seated behind the wheel. "Go back to school, Kidds," he said, although it could've been, "Go back to school, kids." With our name, it gets confusing sometimes.

"Your uncle Timothy would be most displeased," the Asian man continued, "if you were to leave Chumley Prep before the school term is completed."

"Really?" said Tommy. "Then we're *definitely* leaving!"

And we ran even faster down the sidewalk, leaving the car stuck in New York City traffic.

None of us were all that interested in what Uncle Timothy thought about our behavior. We were much more interested in finding Aunt Bela Kilgore (whoever she was) and rescuing Mom!

CHAPTER 13

The next day, we realized something: We should've spent a little more time planning our Great Escape.

Like, maybe even ten minutes.

Because running out of Chumley Prep with nothing but some clothes, a couple of personal items, and very little money was not the smartest way to survive in New York City, one of the most expensive cities on earth.

To make matters even worse, we couldn't even call Professor Lewis, our only friend in

New York City, for a place to stay. We just had no way of really knowing if he'd make us go back to Chumley.

So we aimlessly wandered the streets of Manhattan and ended our dreary day working the crowds outside Grand Central Terminal, the city's major train station. The four of us were hoping to scrape up enough spare change to buy one big salty pretzel we could divvy up for dinner.

While we were busy panhandling, I saw that same black town car that had been parked outside Chumley Prep.

The car was slowly creeping up Forty-Second Street. The driver's window lowered and, once again, I saw the man's face.

"You guys?" I said to my siblings. "It's him!"

"The Asian dude?" said Tommy.

"Yep," said Storm. "Judging by his facial features, his ancestry is most likely from the southern provinces of China."

"Hide!" shouted Tommy.

Tommy, Beck, and I jumped behind a guy walking around with a sandwich board advertising FRIENDLY FOOT RUBS.

Storm dived behind a hot dog cart.

The car kept crawling up the block.

We were okay. Uncle Timothy's friend hadn't spotted us. And, somehow, Storm had scored a hot dog with everything on it.

"It fell to the sidewalk and nearly landed in

a pile of dog poop," she said, chomping a big bite. "The guy said I could take it. Free."

I guess we should've been grossed out, but we were too busy starving.

"Was it on the ground for more than five seconds?" Tommy asked Storm.

"Nope."

"Then let's dig in, guys."

Actually, I don't think the five-second rule applies when you're outdoors—especially if you're on the streets of New York.

But that was how down and desperate we were after just one day.

We split the dirty dog into four more bite-sized chunks and called it dinner.

CHAPTER 14

H ow down were we?

How about all the way down to the subterranean bowels of Grand Central Terminal—down in the tunnels underneath all the other tunnels. Down where rats rule the rails. Starving and exhausted, we ended up calling it a day at the long-abandoned Waldorf-Astoria train platform.

"This is where VIPs used to park their private train cars so they could sneak into the hotel upstairs without anybody seeing them," said our

underground tour guide, Storm. "That train car over there? That was for Franklin Delano Roosevelt when he was president. It was big enough to carry him and his armor-plated Pierce Arrow automobile."

"Cool," said Tommy. "But who's she?" Turns out, we weren't the only ones hiding out underneath Grand Central.

In no time, Tommy flirted his way to friendship with a cute, teenaged runaway named Mildred.

"My friends call me Millie," she said.

We all nodded but, at that moment, none of us really cared. We were too busy staring at the Dunkin' Donuts box. Well, all of us except Tommy. He was staring at Millie.

"I went Dumpster diving earlier," Millie explained. "You guys hungry?"

TOMMY THE FLIRTMEISTER

Hot dogs plucked off the sidewalk and doughnuts scooped out of garbage cans. New York City
has some of the finest food in the world if you're
famished.

Actually, it was really sweet of Millie to share
her dinner.

"So where are you guys running away from?"
Millie asked while we wolfed down her doughnuts.

Tommy gave Millie a grin. "Nowhere. See, we're the Kidds. We don't run *away* from anything. We run *to* action, adventure, and, of course, danger."

"Really? That's awesome. I'm from Plattsburgh, and nothing exciting or dangerous ever happens in Plattsburgh."

Tommy wiggled his eyebrows. "So maybe you'd like to go on an adventure with me to Cairo?"

"Really?" gushed Millie. "Cairo? In Egypt?"

"Is there any other?"

"Yes," said Storm. "Cairo, Illinois."

"Egypt would be soooo totally amazing!" Millie gushed.

Beck and I exchanged a glance.

It was time to school Millie and, simultaneously, save our big brother. From himself.

CHAPTER 15

"You know, Millie," I said, "dangerous adventures aren't for everybody."

"In fact," said Beck, "they can be downright scary."

"Like this one time pirates kidnapped Beck and nearly made her walk the plank."

"Another time," said Beck, "Serbian thugs didn't like us digging up a treasure chest—"

"So," I said, picking up the tale and embellishing it, "they jumped Tommy and tortured him with toothpicks they shoved under his fingernails. Then there was the time our boat was hijacked by masked Malayan marauders—"

"You guys?" said Tommy, hoping we'd stop scaring his new girlfriend.

But I kept going. "Look, Millie, I'm sure Plattsburgh has plenty of nice, safe adventures that'd be totally cool for you. But, if you come with us to Cairo, you'll probably end up with a deadly scorpion inside your shoe. At the very least."

"Don't forget the spiders," said Beck. "The spiders in Egypt are the size of rats."

I nodded. "Only fuzzier and with a lot more legs and poisonous fangs."

Millie's eyes were about to explode out of her face.

"Then, of course," I said, "there are the camel stampedes."

"C-c-camel stampedes?" stammered Millie.

"Oh, yeah. They happen two or three times a day in Cairo. They call it 'Hump Hour.' And it's so crowded there's not even room to get out of the way, so you have to just stand there and hope the camels don't trample you."

Millie had heard enough. "I gotta go!"

Tommy looked heartbroken. "What? Where?"

"Home!"

Millie took off running into the darkness, shrieking every time a rat squeaked at her.

"Why did you guys do that?" grumbled Tommy.

"Because your girlfriends are bad news," said Beck.

"Don't forget," added Storm, "we lost the Twins and all that sunken treasure to Nathan Collier because of Gina, your redheaded friend in the polka-dot bikini."

"So zip it," said Beck.

"Okay," sighed Tommy. "You're right. Besides, I'm too tired to chase after Millie anyway."

"We should get some sleep," I said. "Tomorrow we need to scrape together enough cash to buy four airplane tickets to Egypt."

I pulled Dad's weather-beaten rain slicker out of my backpack, figuring I'd use it as a blanket.

And I'd also make sure he hadn't sewn several thousand dollars into the lining.

Hey, it couldn't hurt to look.

CHAPTER 16

Of course, none of us could really sleep. Trains kept rumbling into the station above us. Beck discovered an orphaned alligator in a nearby sewer pipe. Rats the size of wiener dogs were having some kind of karaoke dance party two tracks over.

And we all kept thinking about Mom and Dad.

Around three in the morning, the four of us huddled in a circle on the abandoned train platform and started swapping stories.

"Hey, Bick, remember that time in New Zealand?" said Beck.

"How could I forget it? Mom and Dad took us to that park where we flew across a canyon on a zip line. Best birthday ever."

"That's because," said Tommy, "we had the best parents ever."

I hugged the rain slicker a little closer. "We still have them, Tommy."

"Yeah," said Beck, surprising me a little. "We just need to find them."

"And rescue them!" I added.

Tommy nodded. "I'm down for that."

"You guys?" said Storm with a heavy sigh. "They're dead. Both of them."

"No, they are *not*," I said. "Would a dead man hide a rain slicker in a secret compartment?"

"Maybe. Right before he was swept overboard and drowned."

"What about this?" said Beck, brandishing the thumb drive. "Mom wasn't dead when she made that video."

Storm shook her head. "Odds are, she is now."

"Hey, Storm?" said Tommy.

"Yeah?"

"Remember that time when you were, like, nine and you were in that sea kayak race down in Guadeloupe?"

"Yeah. I finished last. Three and a half hours after everybody else. It was the day I officially gave up all competitive sports."

"But who was waiting for you at the finish line even though it was dark and raining and everybody else had gone home?"

"Mom and Dad."

"Exactly. So maybe we just need to wait for them a little longer, too."

"Maybe."

And that was about as close as you'll get to a *"Mom and Dad might not be dead"* from Storm.

That is, until six in the morning, when she

92

surprised us all by bellowing out an excited wake-up call.

"'Reading is the key to all of life's treasures!'" Storm shouted. "Remember? That's what was written on the book- mark."

Beck pulled the decorated leather strip out of her bag.

Storm yanked the thing right out of Beck's hand.

OKAY, KIDDS! ENOUGH OF THIS PATHETIC, MOROSE, DEFEATIST DRIBBLE! WE HAVE OTHER OPTIONS! WE JUST NEED TO DO WHAT DAD SAID!

"And look what's tied to the top of the book- mark!" She held it upside down so the tiny key would dangle. "A key! Maybe this is, literally, 'the key to all of life's treasures.'"

"No," said Tommy, pointing to the words punched into the leather. "According to the book- mark, *reading* is the key to everything...."

"Fine," said Storm. "But *this* is a key to a safe-deposit box."

"Really?" I said. "How can you tell?"

"Because I *read* it!"

Storm was right.

We'd found the key to one of the many safe-deposit boxes Mom and Dad kept scattered across the globe.

Why'd they need so many?

To safeguard all sorts of small treasures.

And hopefully to hide treasure maps!

CHAPTER 17

First thing in the morning the four of us trooped into the extremely swanky lobby of the Park Avenue branch of First NYC Bank.

Everyone in the building was wearing a suit or a nice dress.

Well, everyone except us.

It didn't matter. We had the key, which we presented to a snooty man with either a very thin mustache or an extremely skinny caterpillar sleeping on his lip.

"We, um, need to get something out of our, you know, box thingy," said Tommy.

We'd elected Tailspin Tommy to be our spokesperson for the bank excursion because he was the oldest.

We may need to rethink that in the future.

The snooty man sniffed and looked down his nose at our key.

Finally, he said, "My pleasure!" in a British accent and slipped on a pair of starched white gloves. "Follow me."

The banker led us down a glass-and-marble staircase and into a vault where the walls were lined with cabinets of boxes that looked like wider versions of the mailboxes you'd see in the lobby of an apartment building.

Each safe-deposit box door had two key slots. The guy with the white gloves inserted his key into one of the holes on the box labeled 1818; Tommy stuck our key into the other. When they both turned their keys, the door swung open. Tommy took hold of a handle and slid a long metal tray out of the box.

"Would you like a room?" the snooty man asked with another sniff.

"For tonight?" said Tommy. "That'd be awesome. Because right now we're kind of—"

Beck elbowed Tommy in the hip.

"Right now we're kind of in a hurry," Beck said so Tommy wouldn't tell the banker about our temporary sleeping arrangements underneath Grand

Central Terminal. "So, yes, a viewing room would be nice."

"My pleasure."

After Sir Snobbypants set us up in a small conference room and quietly closed the door, Tommy raised the lid on Mom and Dad's box.

Inside were a paperback book, a stack of maps, and a purple velvet jeweler's bag embroidered with loopy lettering that spelled out RONNY VENABLE'S JEWEL AND SOUP EMPORIUM. Tommy grabbed the bag, untied a braided golden string, and tugged open the top.

"Whoa!"

"What's inside?" I asked.

"Someone call the queen of England. I think Mom and Dad found her crown!"

The jeweled headdress was covered with glistening diamonds, green emeralds, and bright red rubies.

Storm moved in for a closer look.

"Actually, Tommy," she said, "I believe this diamond-encrusted diadem originally belonged to the czarina of Russia. It's been missing since 1917, when Czar Nikolai the Second and his wife fled their palace and gave three wooden crates filled with the Russian crown jewels to some monks in the Ural Mountains for safekeeping. A few months later, Bolshevik revolutionaries overran the monks' monastery. The Bolsheviks believed in workers sharing the wealth of the ruling class, so they took the crown jewels from the monks and gave them to a farmer. The farmer hid them and never told anybody where he had hidden the missing crates."

"But Dad found them?" I asked.

"I'd say he found at least one."

"So what's a crown with that many diamonds and jewels worth?" asked Beck, who's usually in charge of all our Kidd family wheeling and dealing.

Storm actually smiled. "Millions."

"Woo-hoo!" I shouted. "We're rich again!"

Beck and I high-fived.

Then we did our special Twins-Only End Zone Dance: We rocked from side to side and did a few "raise the roof" moves.

"Hey, hang on, you guys," Tommy said as he pulled a folded piece of paper out of the bottom of the metal drawer. "This might be worth even more."

"What is it?" I asked.

"A letter from Dad!"

CHAPTER 18

Tommy quickly placed the letter on the table.

"Check out the date," he said. "That's, like, a week before we sailed to Cyprus."

"Cyprus is where Mom got kidnapped!" said Beck, stating the obvious.

(I'm sorry, Beck, but you did. Fine. Draw me with two heads in the next illustration. See if I care.)

"Apparently," said Storm, "Dad must've made a copy of the key we found attached to the bookmark. Then, he came here, right before we shoved off for Cyprus, to tuck that letter into the safe-deposit box."

"Do you think Uncle Timothy sent us to that school so we'd find the bookmark?" I asked.

"Or," said Beck, "maybe Dad knew if he ever went missing, Uncle Timothy would automatically try to dump us in that awful place."

"Either way," I said, "Dad knew—or at least hoped—we'd follow his trail of clues and find his letter."

"Come on, Tommy," said Beck. "Read it."

"Uh, okay." Tommy cleared his throat. "'Dear brilliant children.'"

"That's us!" said Beck.

"'Dear brilliant children. I have never been more proud of the four of you. You have proved yourselves to be true treasure hunters. Congratulations on following the clues that brought you to this box. Unfortunately, I fear you will soon need almost every item inside it—especially if you are here at a time when both your mother and I have gone missing. If that is the case, move swiftly. We don't have much time. And remember—you can trust your uncle Timothy to a point, but *never* trust him with your lives or turn your back on him for too long. Love, Dad.'"

"That's it?" said Beck.

"No. There's a P.S.: 'Keep following the clues. Show the world what Kidds can do.'"

"What clues?"

Storm was sorting through the stuff Tommy had pulled out of the box. "There are four maps in here. All of them for the African treasures

Mom and Dad mentioned. Hey, remember King Solomon's Mines?"

"The book!" I said, pointing to the paperback that had been tucked inside the box. "It's *King Solomon's Mines*!"

"First published in 1885," said Storm, our walking Wikipedia. "It was a bestselling novel by Victorian adventure writer Sir H. Rider Haggard and tells the story of a group of African treasure hunters led by Allan Quatermain."

"So that's a clue," said Beck. "Dad's telling us to go to Africa and find the mines!"

Storm spread out the treasure map leading to King Solomon's Mines.

"Fascinating," said Storm.

"What?" said Tommy.

"Nothing," said Storm. "At least—not yet. I need to do a little more research."

I turned over the velvet jeweler's bag and pointed at the flaking gold imprint on it. "Here's another clue. It's the address for Ronny Venable's Jewel and Soup Emporium here in New York City."

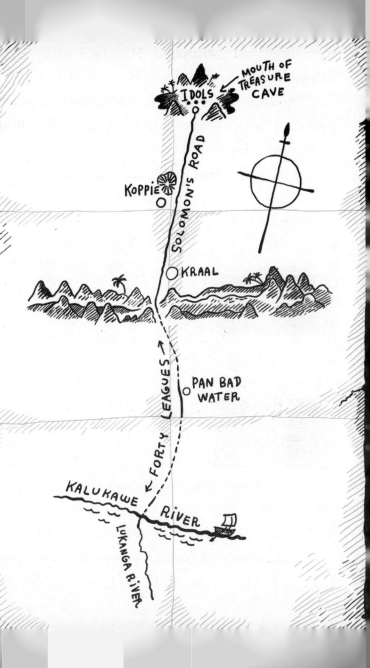

"Check out the shop's slogan," said Beck. "'Always fair. Always beautiful wares.'"

"That same slogan is on this business card," I said. "It was tucked inside the bag. Looks like Dad made a few small edits."

RONNY VENABLE'S
JEWEL & SOUP
EMPORIUM
• DOWNSTAIRS, 2½ BOND STREET, NEW YORK, NY •
-ALWAYS FAIR-   -ALWAYS BEAUTIFUL WARES-

The instant I figured it out, I shouted, "That says 'always be ware'!"

"Thanks for that, Captain Obvious," said Beck.

"Guilty. But look how Dad circled 'always fair.' He's telling us to take the crown to this Venable

106

guy because he'll pay us a fair price. But we need to be extra careful because he might also try to cheat us."

"Don't worry," said Beck, our chief negotiator. "He might try, but he'll definitely fail."

Storm grabbed the four treasure maps and the paperback book. Tommy slid the diamond-encrusted crown back into its velvet bag and stuffed the whole thing inside the hip pocket of his cargo shorts.

We were off to 2½ Bond Street.

If we could sell the Russian crown for a fair price, we'd definitely have enough money to fly to Cairo. And since Mr. Venable also sold soup, we wouldn't have to Dumpster dive for doughnuts at dinnertime!

CHAPTER 19

The Jewel & Soup Emporium was on a pretty sketchy cobblestone street.

We descended a steep set of stairs to enter a basement that reeked of chopped onions and boiled cabbage. Only a few seedy characters—most had scars, tattoos, and those pointy face studs that look like steel pimples—were slurping thick and chunky soups at the rickety tables scattered around the restaurant.

There was no jewelry on display anywhere.

A man I figured was probably Ronny Venable stood behind the cafeteria-style counter, ladling lumpy brown slop into bowls.

The slop smelled like a wet goat. So did Mr. Venable, whose long black hair was greasier than raw strips of bacon.

"What do you kids want? Soup?"

Beck swaggered forward. "Not if today's special is what it smells like: cream of horse manure. But, hey—at least you got our name right."

"What do you mean, kid?"

"That's right. We're the Kidds."

"So?"

"Dr. Thomas Kidd's kids?"

Now Mr. Venable's beady black eyes darted back and forth, sizing us up.

"We brought you something," said Tommy, pulling the velvet bag out of his hip pocket.

"It's a very rare borscht," said Beck, winking to let the shady dude know she was speaking in code.

"Borscht? You brought me a bag of beet soup?"

Beck rolled her eyes. "Noooo. Something much better. Much more *Russian*."

"Goulash?"

"It's not soup, okay?"

Storm stepped forward. "You ever hear about Czar Nikolai the Second and his missing crown jewels?" she whispered.

"Maybe," Venable whispered back.

"Well, sir," she said, "some of them aren't so 'missing' anymore."

CHAPTER 20

Mr. Venable immediately escorted us into a back storage room. The shelves were filled with stacks of jumbo-sized soup cans and display cases filled with sparkling jewels.

"Welcome to my jewel emporium," he said. "Your father was one of my first and best customers. I'm sure we can come to...terms."

Tommy looked around the dingy storeroom. "Um, do you have any money back here?"

Venable tapped a gallon can of cream of spinach soup. Its lid popped open to reveal a stack of crisp one-hundred-dollar bills.

"We're going to need several gallons of 'spinach' to let you have this," said Beck, giving Tommy the go-ahead to pull the jewel-studded crown out of its bag.

The sleazy jeweler gasped and, in no time, he and Beck hammered out a deal that, given our current circumstances, was pretty darn excellent.

First, Mr. Venable agreed to pay us $1 million—fifty thousand in cash for "walking-around money" with the rest to be deposited in a numbered Swiss bank account that he set up using a hidden computer.

"Here are your ATM cards," he said, pulling them out of what looked like a saltine cracker box.

Tommy took the cards and ran up the block to the nearest cash machine to make sure our new bank account wasn't bogus. He came back with a stack of twenty-dollar bills.

"Just in case somebody can't break a Benjamin," he said.

Then, for a "small convenience fee," Mr. Venable arranged first-class plane tickets and hotel accommodations for us in Cairo. Finally, for an additional "airport security fee," the oily dude agreed to fly with us to Egypt as our legal guardian so we wouldn't have to deal with the whole "unaccompanied minor" issue at the airport.

"Do you children need passports?" he asked, eager to make one final sale.

"Nope," I said. "Mom and Dad gave us each a passport on our first birthday and made sure to keep renewing them. It's sort of a Kidd family tradition."

"Then we are all set," said Mr. Venable, rubbing his hands together like a greedy raccoon. "We leave for Cairo on Egypt Air tonight at six thirty. Now, then, who wants soup? No extra charge."

We politely turned down his generous offer.

Hey, we had money again. We could find a Burger King. Nobody was really in the mood for Mr. Venable's barnyard surprise stew.

CHAPTER 21

O kay, this is the part of the story where we, basically, fly to Egypt.

It's an eleven-hour flight and pretty boring unless you really, really, *really* like little bags of salty peanuts and reruns of old TV shows.

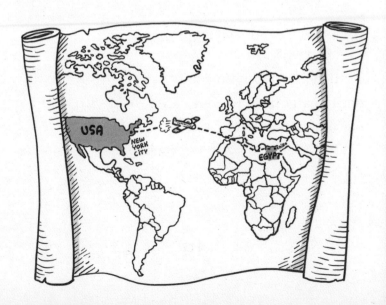

By the way, in case you missed it, those four African treasure maps in the safe-deposit box were for the same four treasures we already talked about:

1. **King Solomon's Mines**
2. **Kruger's Hidden Millions**
3. **The Ming Dynasty Artifacts from Zheng He's Treasure Fleet**
4. **La Buse's (The Buzzard's) Abandoned Pirate Treasure**

Where would you go if you were us? Go ahead, talk it over with your friends. Get your whole class in on the act. Take your time. Like I said, the flight to Cairo is going to take eleven hours.

Oh, right. Duh.

Beck is reminding me that this is a book. I don't really have to wait eleven hours for it to be eleven hours later.

I just have to start a new chapter.

CHAPTER 22

M r. Venable checked us into a deluxe suite at the Mena House hotel in Cairo.

"If you need soup," he said, "give me a call. I packed a couple gallons of chicken noodle in my suitcase."

We told him thanks (but no thanks), and Mr. Venable headed off for the Isis Hotel, where the rooms only cost, like, nineteen dollars a night. "I will be in Cairo visiting friends," he said. "Should you need further assistance..."

Tommy finally slipped him a hundred-dollar bill so he'd go away.

He did.

The Mena House hotel cost a lot more than nineteen dollars a night. In fact, it used to be a hunting lodge for an Egyptian king named Ismail the Magnificent.

We could actually see the Great Pyramid of Cheops from the balcony of our room. It was basking in the sun on the far side of the hotel's golf course.

Yes, it was good to be rich again.

But we weren't interested in playing golf or being pampered poolside. We were in Egypt for one reason and one reason only: to find Mom's mysterious "aunt" Bela Kilgore.

BICK SAYS DAD IS STILL ALIVE. HE IS THE KING OF DENIAL.

Beck and I were sitting on the edge of the sofa in the five-star suite's living room. The rug on the floor looked like it used to belong to Aladdin. I half expected it to start flying.

We were reviewing Mom's thumb-drive video on the room's plasma-screen TV. Beck kept punching Rewind and replaying one bit over and over and over.

Finally, after the umpteenth rewind, Beck tossed the remote control into the sofa cushions. "What does it mean, Bick? All that junk about the four seasons and Julius Caesar and the number thirteen?"

REW 0:13:41

PLEASE GO VISIT MY AUNT BELA KILGORE. SHE'S IN CAIRO. AND REMEMBER, KIDS — WINTER, SPRING, SUMMER, AND FALL, MY AUNT BELA LOVES JULIUS CAESAR AND THE NUMBER THIRTEEN MOST OF ALL.

"It means," said Tommy, coming into the room, "we need to hit the streets of Cairo and find Bela Kilgore."

"Seriously?" said Storm. "We're just going to hike around the streets of Egypt's capital—which, by the way, is home to over sixteen million people—and ask total strangers, 'Hey, have you ever heard of a lady named Bela Kilgore?'"

Tommy thought about that for a second. "Guess we might be here for a while."

"I don't care how long it takes," I said, "or how impossible it seems. We need to find this Bela person so we can help Mom! I really, *really* think 'Aunt' Bela is another CIA spook who worked with Mom."

"We know, Bick," said Beck. "You've told us. Over and over and over."

(It's true. But at least I didn't make warbled rewind noises like that video clip Beck made me watch over and over and over.)

"Come on, you guys," said Tommy. "Let's hit the streets. We have sixteen million people to talk to."

CHAPTER 23

The four of us crowded onto a bus with an eager group of American and British tourists decked out in plaid shorts and sun hats and made the fourteen-kilometer trip from the hotel, across the Nile River, and into the heart of Cairo.

We got off the bus in Tahrir Square, not far from the Egyptian Museum, where treasures from the tomb of King Tut—the boy pharaoh who died when he was just nineteen—are on permanent display, including his famous burial mask, which is made out of 24.5 pounds of pure gold! I read in a book once that King Tut might have been murdered. If that story is true, maybe the bad guys wanted his solid-gold mask.

Anyway, Cairo was a sometimes scary, sometimes cool place.

For instance, in what was called a "legal graffiti zone" near Tahrir Square, the walls were covered with slogans scrawled in Arabic and giant caricatures of the heroes and villains from the Arab Spring uprisings. Beck's favorite, naturally, was the portrait of an artist with a paintbrush standing up to a riot-squad trooper with a billy club. Like I said: cool, but a little scary.

The streets were bustling with people. Donkey carts and taxicabs fought one another for room on the extremely crowded streets.

Storm coached us all to greet everyone we met with a *"Es-Salāmu-Àlĕku,"* which means "Peace be upon you." We also had to smile, she said.

"In Egypt, people who don't smile are considered arrogant, rude, and aggressive."

And so we smiled and asked, "Do you know where we might find a woman named Bela Kilgore?"

The Egyptians we met all smiled back and shook their heads.

Yes, we were basically trying to find a grain of sand in the Sahara Desert.

But the search for "Aunt Bela"—the only clue we had that might, hopefully, lead us to rescuing Mom—kept driving us deeper and deeper into the heart of Cairo.

CHAPTER 24

We ventured into the Khan el-Khalili, one of Cairo's major souks.

A souk is an open-air marketplace or bazaar. Small shops were crowded inside the Khan el-Khalili's ancient fourteenth-century walls. Vendors sat cross-legged in stalls selling all sorts of stuff: brightly colored spices, brass bracelets, teapots, T-shirts, postcards, and souvenirs.

"The Khan el-Khalili dates back to 1382," said Storm. "At one time, this marketplace also had a monopoly on all the spices moving from the

Eastern World into the West. This single souk's stranglehold on the spice trade is why Columbus set sail to the West, hoping to find an alternate route to the East."

The market was a chaotic maze of narrow alleys. All around us, I could hear goldsmiths hammering out trinkets and rings as shopkeepers hawked their wares and haggled over prices.

But what really struck me was the number of street children running around without any parents. A lot of them were my age or younger. All of them looked like they were starving.

Remember, not too long ago, the four of us had basically been street urchins outside Grand Central Terminal—homeless beggars eating doughnuts out of garbage cans.

So we invited a group of kids to join us in a café, where we all feasted on sticky sesame bars and basboussa (cake soaked with syrup).

As we were finishing up our Egyptian pastries with our new friends, a mysterious man in a

tasseled red fez (a felt hat that sort of looked like an upside-down sand bucket) approached our table.

"Excuse me, are you by any chance the Kidd children?" he asked as he stroked his chin thoughtfully.

"Who wants to know?" said Tommy, standing up from the table.

"I am Makalani." Our visitor bowed slightly

and touched the chest of his robe, where I noticed a stain and squiggly piece of dry pasta. Apparently, Mr. Makalani was a messy eater. I could relate.

"I trust you are enjoying your time in Cairo?" he said with a smile. He was missing a couple of teeth.

"The pastries are good," said Beck, licking her fingers to make sure she got every particle of powdered sugar.

"And our hotel is awesome!" I said.

"Extremely swanky," added Tommy. "The Mena House out by the pyramids. Ever heard of it?"

"Oh, yes. Very, very nice. Your mother's aunt Bela would be most pleased."

"Wait a second," I said. "You know Bela Kilgore?"

The man in the fez smiled. "Oh, yes, Kidd children. I know many, many things. Many, many people."

CHAPTER 25

"Where is she?" demanded Beck, forgetting all that stuff about "peace be upon you" Storm had taught us earlier.

"Ah—you are eager to find this Bela Kilgore, yes?"

"Yes!"

Makalani licked his lips as if they were dry.

"I am told the coffee in this café is quite good. The baklava pastries as well."

Tommy whipped out a crisp one-hundred-dollar bill. "You tell us how to find Bela Kilgore and you can buy yourself a gallon of espresso and a couple of those fruity cream pies in the window, too."

"You are most generous. Therefore, it is my humble pleasure to inform you that you will find your mother's aunt Bela at the Giza pyramids, so very near your current hotel accommodations. She is, as they say, undercover—pretending to work at the Great Pyramids as a tour guide."

"But she's really with the CIA?" I blurted out. "Right?"

Beck kicked my shin under the table.

Makalani raised both shoulders and held out his hands. "More than what I have already told you I cannot say."

131

For a second the Egyptian in the Shriner hat reminded me of Yoda.

Makalani plucked the one-hundred-dollar bill out of Tommy's hand. "Enjoy your visit to the pyramids, Kidd children. I trust it will be very... *educational. Maa salama.* Go with safety."

He bowed again, backed out of the coffee shop, and vanished into the teeming throngs on the sidewalk.

"We need to catch that bus back to the hotel," said Tommy. "Now!"

"Wait a second," said Beck, gesturing toward our wide-eyed young guests, still crowded around the table. "You have another one of those Benjamins?"

"Yeah," I said. "These guys need to have a good dinner to go with their dessert."

"Maybe a little lamb kebab, baba ghanoush, samak makli, and tahini?" added Storm, who sometimes uses her photographic memory to memorize menus.

Tommy winked. "Definitely."

In fact, he gave the kids *two* one-hundred-dollar bills.

They danced in the streets with joy; we headed back to Giza to see two of the Seven Wonders of the World.

The Great Pyramids and Bela Kilgore—the lady all of us were wondering about!

CHAPTER 26

A very happy man running a cart in the bazaar arranged a camel tour of the Giza pyramids for us with a young guide who, he said, "knows everything and everybody."

So the four of us climbed aboard our hump-backed so-called ships of the desert and made ourselves as comfortable as you can in a Bedouin saddle—which is basically a clunky wooden chair resting on top of the camel's hump and a brightly colored, braided blanket with lots of dangling tassels that look like extra camel tails.

"Follow me, if you please, Kidds," said our tour guide, Bubu, a wiry boy about my age in a turban and a loose-fitting, long shirt. His camel's saddle had more brightly colored pom-poms and decorations than any of ours. "I will show you all three pyramids, the great and mighty Sphinx, even the tomb of Queen Hetepheres! Might I remind you that tipping of your tour guide is greatly appreciated? I will accept shoes, watches, jewelry, and even cash."

I felt a little sorry for Storm's camel. She knew more about the pyramids than the camel did, even though the camel had taken the tour with Bubu a billion times. It must have been horrible for the poor camel's self-esteem.

"Did you know," said Storm, "that it took over twenty years to build the Great Pyramid of Cheops? It is the oldest of the Seven Wonders of the Ancient World and the only one still largely intact."

Storm's camel bellowed sort of like a Wookie.

I think he was as bored as I was, but, hey, this is invaluable material to help your teachers rationalize why our adventure is okay for you to read in school. It might even be worthy of a

classroom discussion or a project. You could make a pyramid out of sugar cubes and Elmer's Glue. Just don't do it outside unless you want ants to attend your miniature pharaoh's funeral.

Anyway, Storm babbled on.

"Due to the angle of the sides in relation to its latitude, the Great Pyramid casts no shadow at noon during the spring equinox...."

"So, Bubu," Beck called out to our tour guide, more or less cutting Storm off before I fell asleep and tumbled off my camel saddle. "Have you ever heard of another tour guide named Bela Kilgore?"

"I'm afraid I do not know of her. I hope this will in no way affect my tip?"

"If you knew how to find Bela Kilgore," I said, "your tip would be huge."

"I see. And what can you tell me of this woman?"

"Not much," said Beck. "Only that she loves Julius Caesar."

"Is that so?" said Bubu. "You know, I have heard that Julius Caesar was a great admirer of Pharaoh Cheops." I figured Bubu was trying to outdo Storm in the pyramid-trivia department.

"Who says that?" asked Storm.

"Many, many intelligent people. They tell me that Julius Caesar used to sneak into the tomb of the pharaoh with Cleopatra when the two of them were dating. There are many secret tunnels and passageways for royals seeking privacy."

Storm blew out her lips and made a camel noise. "Bull hockey," she said.

"Oh, no. This is very, very true. Like your Bela Kilgore, Queen Cleopatra loved Julius Caesar."

Beck and I shot each other a glance.

"Would perhaps you four wish to explore the insides of the pyramid to see if what I say is true?" asked Bubu. "It can be arranged. For a non-refundable fee, of course."

"Let's do it," I said.

Hey, it was worth a shot. So far, it was our only connection between Egypt and Julius Caesar. Besides, what'd we have to lose poking around inside a pyramid?

CHAPTER 27

"**P**lease remove your shoes before entering the Great Pyramid of Khufu," said Bubu, who was holding the reins to all four camels outside the entrance.

"Seriously?" said Tommy. He was sporting an awesome new pair of Nikes.

"It is customary when entering a mosque," said Storm, "to remove any shoes, sandals, boots, or slippers. They carry dirt from the street."

"Um, is the pyramid a mosque?" asked Beck.

"No," said Bubu, "but, for many Egyptians, it is a holy and sacred place."

"Then how come all these other tourists are wearing shoes?"

"I suspect they were raised, as you say, in a barn."

"Come on, you guys," I said, peeling off my sneaks. "We need to hustle. Mom's aunt Bela could be inside."

"Oh, yes," said Bubu. "Now that I think on it, there *is* a woman named Bela who sells Julius Caesar souvenirs down in the subterranean chamber."

Tommy, Storm, and Beck quickly pulled off their shoes, too.

"I will wait here with the camels," said Bubu. "Good luck on your quest to find your lady friend."

We ducked our heads and entered the long, cramped passageway that reminded me of a shaft

in a coal mine, except the walls were brown instead of black. There was a path of wooden planks on the ground, and the tunnel was well lit—so you could see just how cramped and claustrophobic it was.

To reach the subterranean chamber where Bubu said Bela Kilgore had set up shop, we would need to work our way down what is known as the Descending Passage.

But there was a velvet rope blocking access to it.

"The general public is not allowed into the subterranean chamber," said a semiofficial-looking Egyptian in a military shirt and beret. He also looked like he hadn't shaved in maybe a week.

"We're looking for Bela Kilgore," I said. "We're with Bubu. The tour guide?"

"Oh," said the military man, his eyes darting back and forth. "Bubu? Why did you not say so in the first place?" He took one last look around, then raised the velvet rope. "Hurry. *Maa salama*. Go with safety."

We began our descent to the restricted room underneath the colossal pyramid.

"When we reach the bottom," said Storm, "there will be two million blocks of stone weighing six-and-a-half-million tons over our heads."

"Good to know," said Beck.

Finally, after practically duckwalking down the cramped corridor, we stepped into the subterranean chamber.

You guessed it.

The room was completely empty.

CHAPTER 28

Breathing hard, we raced back up the tight passageway.

When we reached the velvet rope, the so-called security guard wasn't there anymore.

"You think the guard and Bubu were working together?" I wondered out loud.

"Well, duh!" said Beck. "Bubu sent us into that pyramid pit on a wild-goose chase."

"What?" said Tommy. "Why?"

"I'm not sure, but I have a hunch."

We stepped out of the pyramid and into the blindingly bright sun.

Bubu was gone. Our camels were gone.

"My Nikes!" groaned Tommy.

And, yes, our shoes were gone, too.

"We got played," said Storm, who, from the look in her eyes, was revisiting everything she remembered about our guide. "Bubu only said all that stuff about Julius Caesar after we fed him the information about Aunt Bela and Caesar."

"Wow," said Tommy. "Do we still have to tip him?"

"No way," said Beck. "But we do have to hike back to our hotel."

The Mena House wasn't very far away, but the walk would've been even easier with shoes.

Eventually, we made it back to the luxurious grounds of our posh hotel.

BEWARE, CHILDREN. LOOKS CAN BE DECEIVING. ESPECIALLY DURING A DANGEROUS ADVENTURE.

"Now what do we do?" I mumbled as we made our way from the gardens into the hotel's elegant hallways.

"Put on other shoes," said Tommy. "Good thing I packed, like, six pairs of kicks."

The instant Tommy opened the door to our suite, all of us stopped worrying about our missing shoes.

Because our hotel room was beyond trashed.

CHAPTER 29

While we were off in Cairo and riding camels and hiking down to the subterranean chamber of the Great Pyramid, somebody had rifled through everything in our room.

Lamps were knocked over. Drawers were flung open. Clothes were scattered everywhere.

"W-w-what kind of inhuman, lowlife scum would do this?" I stammered when I discovered what was missing in the living room. "They stole the thumb drive with Mom's video!"

"The map to King Solomon's Mines is gone,

too!" reported Beck, who'd been checking the hotel closet safe. Its door had been crowbarred off its hinges.

"What about the other three maps?" I asked.

"I have them," said Storm, patting a pocket.

"What? Why'd you only take three?" Beck demanded. "The thieves stole the most important one: the map that went with the *King Solomon's Mines* paperback book Dad hid in the safe-deposit box!"

"I have my reasons."

"What reasons?"

"I'll tell you later."

"Later?" Beck was turning a shade a purple very similar to that of an eggplant. "Later will be too late!"

Tommy stepped between Storm and Beck. "You guys? We need to focus our energies on what's important. Finding Bela Kilgore. Rescuing Mom."

Here's a shocker: When Tommy said that, he sounded exactly like our dad. When things got tough, Dad always kept calm and carried on.

"I know you're upset, Beck," Tommy continued. "You too, Storm, even though, you know, you do a better job of hiding it. But, remember—we'll get through this thing—if we stick together."

Beck raised her hand.

"Yeah?" said Tommy.

"Is this, like, the new you or something?"

"Maybe."

"Good. Because it's kind of sweet."

"Yeah," said Storm. "It's almost as if Dad were still here."

Suddenly it struck me: "This is why Dad told us to 'be ware' of that soup dude, Mr. Venable!"

"Huh?" said Tommy.

"On the business card. He scratched out those letters so we'd know to 'be-ware' of the sleazy jeweler. Okay—remember that guy Makalani in the market café? The one who told us that Bela Kilgore was a tour guide at the Giza pyramids?"

"Yes," said Storm as she called up her photographic memory of the encounter. "He had a food stain on his robe. Soup and a dried noodle."

"Exactly! Chicken noodle! He was working for Venable. I bet Bubu was working for him, too. And that fake security guard inside the pyramid probably does the shoe scam with Bubu at least twice a day!"

"But why?" asked Beck.

"Because somebody really doesn't want us finding Aunt Bela!"

"Who?"

"Whoever's paying Mr. Venable more than we did!"

CHAPTER 30

The burglars had made a rock-stars-on-tour mess when they ransacked our hotel room, but they hadn't stolen anything except the thumb drive and treasure map.

Not even the stack of cash sitting in the busted-open closet safe.

That bit of good luck didn't stop Beck and me from launching into Twin Tirade No. 464.

"So now what?" Beck started. "We go back to interviewing every single person in Cairo?"

"If that's the only way we have to find Bela Kilgore," I said, "then yes."

"That's ridiculous."

"No, it's not."

"Okay, it's impossible."

"Wrong again, Rebecca. It just isn't easy."

"Oh. You're saying I'm lazy?"

"You said it, not me."

"Grow up, Bickford."

"I can't, unless you grow up, too. We're twins, remember?"

153

"This is like looking for a black cat in a coal mine, a drop in a bucket..."

I jumped in with my own simile: "It's like looking for a needle in a haystack!"

"Okay, Bickford, that's just stupid. Why would anybody ever look for a needle in a haystack?"

"It's an official cliché, Rebecca."

"You mean a stupid cliché. How do you lose a needle in a haystack? Who does their sewing anywhere near hay?"

"I don't know. Maybe that's why you can't ever find a needle in a haystack."

Beck nodded. "Maybe so. Good point."

"Well, you brought it up first."

"Thanks."

"No problem."

"We done?"

"Totally."

Tommy and Storm came into the living room.

"You guys," said Tommy, still sounding extremely Dad-like, "we need to switch hotels."

"This one has been compromised," added Storm.

"I can pack in five minutes," I said.

"I can do it in three," said Beck.

"But where should we go?" I asked.

"Well," said Tommy, "according to a couple of websites I checked out, there are other top-notch hotels in Cairo. All of them give you a free bath-robe."

For some reason, this was important to Tommy. Probably because he spends so much time in the morning in front of the mirror.

"There's the Kempinski Nile, the Fairmont, the Sofitel, the Four Seasons..."

"Of course!" I yelled as everything came together. "That's where Aunt Bela is!"

"Huh?"

"The Four Seasons hotel! That's why Mom said that stuff about 'winter, spring, summer, and fall' in the video. Those are the four seasons. She knew exactly where Aunt Bela would be staying in Cairo."

We grabbed a cab and headed to the Nile Plaza, where Cairo's Four Seasons hotel was, to play my hunch.

Tommy gave the bellman who opened our cab

door a hefty tip. Make that massive: $300.

It was enough to buy us the room number to Bela Kilgore's suite.

"But beware," whispered the cooperative bell-man. "You are not the only ones looking for her."

He tapped his shirt pocket. It was stuffed with cash.

CHAPTER 31

We took the hotel elevator up to the twenty-second floor and banged on Bela's door.

"Aunt" Bela didn't look much like a spy. She was shorter than Beck and me and wore glasses with lenses so thick they made her eyeballs look like gigantic olives.

"We're the Kidds," said Tommy. "Tommy, Storm, Beck, and Bick."

Bela Kilgore wasn't very happy to see any of us.

"How did you children find me?"

"It wasn't easy," said Tommy. "Plus it cost me my brand-new Nikes."

Bela Kilgore's eyes started bulging out of their sockets like one of those rubbery panic dolls you squeeze. "Does your strange uncle Timothy know where I am?"

"I doubt it," said Beck. "Heck, he doesn't even know where *we* are."

"Quick question," I said. "Are you 'related' to Uncle Timothy? Are you another CIA contact for our mom?"

She gasped. "How did you figure that out?"

"Well, the whole uncle/aunt thing made it kind of easy."

Now her eyes darted back and forth. "Very well.

158

You children are as clever and cunning as your parents. I might as well tell you the truth. Yes! I manage your mother's missions!"

"Boom!" I said, doing an arm chug. "Nailed it! I *knew* you helped Mom. But *noooooo*. Everybody else—"

Bela cut me off. "Did anyone follow you children here?"

"Maybe," said Tommy. "The bellhop dude downstairs is making a ton of cash giving people your room number."

"The bellhop..." Bela muttered, picking up a designer leather backpack and strapping the dainty thing over her shoulders.

"Going somewhere?" said Beck.

"Yes, and so should you. Leave here, children. Immediately! Go far, far, far away! Otherwise, you will blow my cover, and if my cover is blown, there will be dire consequences—not just for me, but for all of western civilization. If my true identity is discovered by certain interested parties, it could threaten the security of the Free World!"

Tommy was impressed. "Whoa. Seriously?"

"Look, Kidds, I know what I just said sounds absurd."

"Uh, yeah," said Beck.

"It's, like, dialogue from a James Bond movie," I said. "One of the lamer ones, too."

"It doesn't matter what you foolish children think," Bela snapped as she backed up toward the giant windows overlooking the Nile River, twenty-two stories below. "You're just kids. You know nothing about the real world. Your mother and father would agree. So just go away."

I moved closer. "Is our mom alive?"

"Go away, little boy."

"Not until you tell us the truth. Yes or no? Is our mother still alive?"

Bela reached over her shoulder and yanked a pen out of her leather backpack. "This pen is actually a mini–rocket launcher capable of shooting a high-powered explosive accurately up to forty yards."

Tommy chuckled. "That's from James Bond, too, right? Are those sofa cushions actually multiple ejector seats?"

"Go away, Kidds. You bother me."

"Tell us the truth," I demanded. "Is our mother still in Cyprus?"

"Just go away!"

Now Beck moved in on Bela, too. "Are you ever honest with anyone about anything?"

"All the time. Let me demonstrate: I honestly want you children to go away. Now."

Beck kept pressing. "What's up with Julius Caesar and the number thirteen?"

"Go! A! Way!"

Now Storm jumped in. "Where'd you get that dive watch?"

"What?" Bela fidgeted with the watchband, which was way too loose on her bony wrist.

"It's a Breitling Superocean Heritage Chronograph, correct?" said Storm. "Did our mother give it to you?"

And finally, Bela Kilgore told us the truth: "Yes!"

CHAPTER 32

B ela Kilgore worked Mom's dive watch off her wrist.

"Here—take it," she said, tossing the watch to Storm. "It doesn't match my backpack."

Okay, I had to wonder: How could this tiny, bad-tempered, nearsighted woman be our athletic, smart, and incredibly savvy mom's boss? Our mom was way too cool for Bela.

"You're Storm, correct?" she said as Storm examined the watch.

"Yep."

"Well, your mother specifically told me to give that watch to Storm if ever we met. Under the circumstances of our meeting, I was initially hesitant to hand it over."

Suddenly there was a knock on the door.

"Room service," said a thickly accented voice in the hall.

Bela's eyes went buggy again. "I didn't order room service!"

"Me neither," said Tommy. "But I am kind of hungry."

Another knock. "Ms. Kilgore? I have your hummus and baba ghanoush."

Now Bela squinted. "I didn't order hummus. Or baba ghanoush!"

She spun around and kicked at the huge window.

"Hiya!"

Glass crackled and showered out of the frame. Loose papers and flower petals were sucked through the gaping hole where the windowpane used to be.

I heard two soft pops in the hallway—*Thwick! Thwick!*

The doorknob tumbled out of the door.

Bela Kilgore leaped out the window.

The bottom of her designer leather back-pack exploded with fire, and she rocketed across the sky.

"Awesome!" said Tommy. "It's a CIA jet pack!"

Thwick! Thwick!

"Um, somebody's shooting at the door," said Beck as a dead bolt lock went flying across the room.

"Sounds like they're using a silencer," said

Storm as she tucked Mom's dive watch into the pocket of her cargo shorts.

Meanwhile, outside, Bela Kilgore's jet pack started sputtering as it careened wildly like a balloon losing all its air. I saw her spiral into a nosedive, then crash with a splash and a sizzle into the Nile River.

Did she live? Did she die?

I couldn't really tell.

Plus we were kind of busy.

Because somebody holding a long-muzzled pistol kicked open the hotel suite door.

It was a man in an eye patch with a pencil-thin mustache who happened to be wearing a French Foreign Legion hat. It had to be Guy Dubonnet Merck, the man our mother had warned us about in her video!

MEET GUY DUBONNET MERCK.
BTW: "MERCK" RHYMES WITH "JERK".

CHAPTER 33

As Guy Dubonnet Merck strode into the hotel suite, I remembered what our mother had said about the skeevoid in her video: "If you ever meet him, run away! Tell Aunt Bela to run away, too."

I sort of wished we all had designer leather backpacks like Aunt Bela's. The kind with rockets inside.

Merck tucked his smoldering pistol into a holster hanging over his khaki army shorts. With his Foreign Legion hat, tan military shirt straight out of World War II, and socks that were rolled back just below his knee, the mustachioed man in the eye patch looked like an evil Boy Scout leader from France.

"*Excusez-moi*, children," he said in a very thick French accent. "Where is Mademoiselle Kilgore?"

"She flew the coop," I said. "Literally."

Merck marched over to the shattered window and gazed out—the wind whipping through the gaping hole ruffled his billowy shorts and made his eye patch flap.

"*C'est bon.* An ambulance crew is fishing her body out of the Nile."

"Is she dead?" asked Beck.

"*Oui.* I believe so."

"You m-m-*murdered* her," Beck stammered.

Merck turned from the blasted-open window and tsk-tsked. "Little girl! *Murdered* is such an ugly word. I prefer *eliminated*. Now, then—did Mademoiselle Kilgore tell you children anything about your *maman* before she, as you say, 'flew the coop'?"

"Our mother?" I said. "No."

I can fib fast.

"*Merveilleux!* I have earned my fee."

"What exactly do you want here, Merck?" demanded Tommy.

"You know my name?"

"Of course," I said. "Our mother told us all about you!"

"Ah, yes. You see, little Kidds, I was and remain your parents' worst nightmare: a ruthless treasure hunter who will stop at nothing, I repeat, *nothing*, to obtain that which I desire. Your parents? Ha! They think they are so smart. They think they can outwit me? Pah!"

He actually spit on the hotel carpet.

"I laugh at explorers such as they who would spend so much time reading the books and doing the research. Books? They are boring. Research? It is worse. Reckless adventure? That, *mes amis*, is exciting. You may quote me."

With the way Merck was throwing around his French, it was a good thing our parents

homeschooled us in at least a half-dozen languages.

"You're not our 'friend,' *mon ami*," Beck piped up.

"And we won't be quoting you anytime soon," Storm chimed in.

ALL BOOKS ARE FOR DUMMIES!

Merck squinted at us with his one good eye. "Now then, little Kidds, tell me, how did you four make your way to Cairo? I am given to understand that your Uncle Timothy now controls your family fortune."

"We stowed away," I said, because one lie usually leads to another. "On an empty oil tanker. It
was the USS *Hess Truck* sailing out of Newark,
New Jersey, on its way to Saudi Arabia for a quick
refill. When the tanker reached the Suez Canal,
we shinnied down the anchor chains and swam
ashore."

"We've come to Africa to find King Solomon's Mines," blurted Storm.

"Ah-hah!" said Merck. "What I have been told is true. You imbecilic children are attempting to take over your parents' treasure-hunting business?"

He shook his head and tsk-tsked again.

"*Sacre bleu*. Children can be so...so...*childish*!

But, tell me, young and foolish Kidds, how do you intend to find King Solomon's Mines without... *this!*"

With a very dramatic flourish, the Frenchman whipped a familiar-looking document out of his breast pocket.

It was our treasure map.

The one Merck had stolen when he ransacked our hotel room.

CHAPTER 34

Just so you know—when Mom and Dad home-schooled us aboard *The Lost*, they didn't just make us book smart about math, science, literature, and foreign languages.

They also gave us diving lessons, music lessons, martial arts training, and, believe it or not, acting lessons. Trust me, acting is a very valuable skill. Especially when you want to fool someone into thinking you desperately need the treasure map he has stolen when all you really need is your big sister's photographic memory of that same map.

So we put on quite a show for Guy Dubonnet Merck.

BICK is SUCH A HAM. HE SHOULDN'T GET TOO CLOSE TO A PILE OF GREEN EGGS.

"We're doomed," I said. "This clever French guy—"

Merck shook his head. "It is pronounced 'ghee.'"

"This clever French guy *ghee* has clearly outwitted us."

"This stupid trip to Cairo was a waste of time," said Beck, playing along.

"It was?" said Tommy.

Beck and I are such good actors we can even

fool Tommy sometimes (not that it's all that hard to do).

"Yes, Tommy," I said. "We're simply no match for Monsieur Merck. He is so clever, cunning, and crafty."

"It is true," said Merck, proudly. "I am all of these things you say."

"This will be the Kidd family's final adventure," said Beck, making it sound like she was about to sob. "Our final failure."

"We should go home," I said, pretending to choke up a little, too. I even bit a knuckle. "Except, we don't really have a home anymore, do we?"

"No," said Tommy, sounding very sad. And he wasn't acting, either. "We don't."

"And we're broke," added Beck.

"What?" said Merck. "What about all those one-hundred-dollar bills I saw stacked inside your hotel room safe?"

"Gone," I said, with a head nudge toward Tommy. "*Someone* likes to gamble. At the racetrack. He kept picking the wrong camel."

"This is very sad for me to hear," said Merck. "I may be ruthless and heartless, but that does not mean I do not have a heart."

(Well, actually, it kind of does, but I wasn't about to contradict him.)

"Inwardly, I weep for you and your misfortune," Merck continued. "Therefore, Kidd children, I will help you abandon your foolish quest to find King Solomon's Mines. I will give you enough money to make your way back to America, where, your uncle Timothy will welcome you with open arms!"

"How do you know our uncle Timothy?" I asked.

"He is, how you say, an *acquaintance*. Of course, I cannot fly you first class on Egypt Air, like certain soup merchants…"

"You know Mr. Venable, too?"

"Monsieur, I am Guy Dubonnet Merck! I know *everybody*!"

I figured he paid Venable to have Makalani send us on that wild-goose chase around the pyramids while he trashed our room and tracked down Bela Kilgore for himself.

"Rejoice, *mes amis*—I shall pay for your safe return home."

"Thank you, kind sir!" I faked it good.

"If, of course, you do not mind traveling in steerage. On a friend of mine's cattle boat. You will have to share two stalls. Boys in one, girls in the other."

"But," I said, "it'll be a grand adventure! Maybe our most exciting journey ever. I'll keep a diary like the sailor in *Two Years Before the Mast*, that book Dad loved so much. I hope it's nothing but heavy seas, strong gales, and frequent squalls of hail and snow."

"Books," sniffed Merck. "Pah! Again I say: They are nothing but a waste of time."

I laid it on even thicker.

"You are so right. Thank you, thank you, Guy Dubonnet Merck. You have turned our pathetic and hopeless lives around. You have saved the Kidd family from certain destruction. Plus, you have told us the truth about reading and how worthless it is."

Merck smiled smugly and gave us four hundred dollars in soggy, crinkled bills.

"Present yourselves to Captain Jacques of the livestock vessel known as *La Vache de la Mer* in the port of Cairo first thing tomorrow morning. Tell him you are to be his manure-mucking crew for the voyage back to America."

"We will, sir," I said, gushing with gratitude.

Merck tipped his Foreign Legion cap at us. "And now, *les misérables* Kidds, I must bid you *adieu*. I, unlike you, have treasure to hunt!"

CHAPTER 35

The instant Merck was out the door, Beck basically went ballistic.

"Okay, Storm—why'd you tell Merck the Jerk that we were heading off to find King Solomon's Mines?!"

"I have my reasons."

"Mind sharing them?"

Storm stared. "Yes."

"You guys?" said Tommy, sounding a lot less like Dad than he had earlier. "Um, I'm starting to wonder, maybe we should cut our losses and call it quits."

"You mean give up on finding Mom and Dad?" I said.

"No. Not, you know, totally. But, dudes." He gestured toward the broken window and the bullet-riddled hotel room door. "This just went beyond dangerous. It's all the way to, you know—whatever's worse."

"Lethal, deadly, or mortiferous," said Storm, who memorized the dictionary when she was three. "Excuse me. I need to examine our new clue."

She pulled Mom's dive watch out of her cargo shorts pocket.

"How is that a clue?" demanded Beck, who was still pretty upset with Storm for blurting out that bit about King Solomon's Mines to Merck, and doubly mad that Storm wouldn't tell her anything about her mysterious "reasons." I could tell. It's a twin thing.

Storm ignored Beck and pushed two buttons on either side of the dive watch's time-setting knob.

The crystal popped open.

So did the face!

"It's a secret compartment," said Storm. "Mom showed me how it works last year. She used to keep her breath strips in here, in case she needed to talk to some high-level government official about a rare artifact. She liked having fresh, minty breath when she did that."

"What's in there now?" I asked.

"Hang on." Storm used the tweezers from her Swiss Army knife to extract a minuscule slip of paper. She tucked the tweezers back into the knife body and flipped open its magnifying glass. "It's some kind of coded message."

Storm squinted and read whatever was written on the paper scrap, which was about the size of a quarter.

"I knew it!" she said with a smile.

"Knew what?" asked Tommy.

"This."

She handed the magnifying glass and secret note to Tommy, who stared at it for a while, then looked even more confused than usual.

Beck and I were up next.

Here's what we saw in extremely tiny type:

Zl fzneg naq jbaqreshy puvyqera! Zl pncgbef urer va Plcehf

ner jvyyvat gb frg zr serr vs Ibh oevat gurz n Zvat Qlanfgl

infr gb tb jvgu gur Terpvna hea gurl npdhverq sebz Ibhe

svefg nqiragher. Tb gb jurer Ibhe qnq gbyq Ibh gb ybbx va

Nsevpn! Ohg or pnershy. Bguref jvyy gel gb fgbc Ibh sebz

frggvat zr serr.

"What is it?" said Beck. "German? Bulgarian?"

I tried, too: "Martian?"

"None of the above," said Storm. She plucked the paper scrap from between my fingers, popped it into her mouth, munched twice, and swallowed.

"Um, I thought that was, like, a superimportant clue?" said Beck.

"It was and still is. But I already memorized it."

"You guys?" said Tommy. "We need to take a family vote. Like, right now."

"Um, what are our choices?" I asked.

"Keep dodging Mr. Merck's bullets here in Africa. Or, maybe, I don't know—we could head up to Cyprus. Try to negotiate some sort of deal with Mom's kidnappers."

"I guess we could also go back to Chumley Prep," mumbled Storm.

"No!" said Beck. "That's nonnegotiable."

"Fine," I said. "We can vote. But before we do, let me remind you guys—we are *The Kidds*. We live for action, adventure, and boldly risking everything for half a chance at some incredible, unknown reward! And one day, I promise—one of these wild and daring adventures is gonna lead us straight to Mom and Dad!"

And so we voted.

As usual, it was unanimous.

We would continue our African adventure, no matter how dangerous or mortiferous it became.

(I don't know what the heck it means, Beck. Ask Storm.)

PART 2

BUNGLE
IN THE
JUNGLE

CHAPTER 36

As soon as the vote was over, Beck and I erupted into Twin Tirade No. 465 about which of the other African treasures we should go searching for now that Merck had a head start to King Solomon's Mines.

"We need to head to Johannesburg," said Beck. "Kruger's gold is just sitting there, waiting for us."

"No," I shouted. "The Buzzard's Abandoned Pirate Treasure is better!"

"What about the Ming Dynasty Artifacts

from Zheng He's Treasure Fleet?" asked Tailspin Tommy, butting into our Twin Tirade.

"Excuse me?" said Beck. "Are you a twin?"

"Um, no…"

"Then stay out of this!" we shouted together.

"Actually," said Storm, "we should continue our quest to find King Solomon's Mines."

That snapped Beck and me out of our tirade instantly.

"What?" said Beck. "Are you nuts? Merck has the treasure map and a head start."

"I'm not worried about Merck," said Storm. "I'm more concerned about whomever he's working for. Whoever hired him to terminate Bela Kilgore in an attempt to stop *us* from finding the secret clue hidden inside Mom's dive watch."

"Yeah!" said Tommy. "Yeah, I don't like that guy, either." He paused for a beat. "Who is he again? The bad guy who hired Merck?"

"I don't know," said Storm. "Not yet. But don't forget—Dad stashed the paperback version of *King Solomon's Mines* in the safe-deposit box, too."

"Um, you guys?" I said, peering out through the shattered window. "Not to be a nag, but can we discuss this someplace else?"

Down below, I could hear the *ee-oo, ee-oo* of approaching police vehicles. I also noticed several people pointing up at the twenty-second floor.

We needed to flee the Four Seasons hotel—like, five minutes ago!

CHAPTER 37

We took the stairs.

But when we hit the lobby, we told Housekeeping Room 2222 needed "a little work."

Like right away.

We hurried to a nearby café to plot our next moves.

As crazy as it sounds, Storm kept insisting that we continue on our mission to find King Solomon's Mines.

"Um, Storm?" said Tommy. "Guy Dubonnet Merck has that treasure map. We don't."

"Yes, we do." She tapped her head. Then she

plucked a paper napkin from the table dispenser, pulled out a pen, and sketched the whole thing from memory.

"Well, where exactly is this Kalukawe River?" said Tommy, tapping the napkin. "I've never seen it on any real map."

"It's in a raised valley, lush and green, in what was once known as Kukuanaland."

"Well," asked Beck, rolling her eyes, "what's it known as now?"

"I'm not sure. But it lies forty leagues north of the Lukanga River in modern Zambia, which would place it in the extreme southeast corner of the Democratic Republic of the Congo."

"And how far away is that?" asked Tommy.

"Two thousand three hundred and twenty-seven miles. We'll need to travel south from Cairo, cross the Nubian Desert, and head to Khartoum. Then come Ethiopia, Kenya, Tanzania, Malawi, and Zambia."

"Why don't we just fly to Zambia?" asked Beck.

Storm shook her head. "Bad idea."

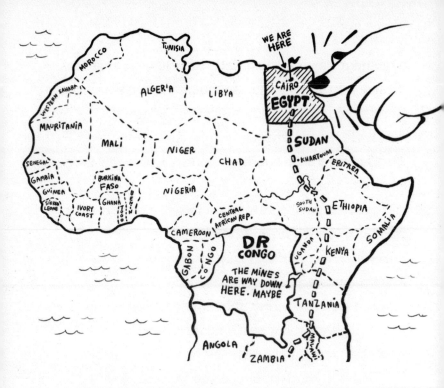

"Really? And driving over two thousand miles across the desert and through the jungle is a good one?"

"It's the smartest move we can make. Trust me, you guys."

Storm had a pleading look in her eyes.

Something in Mom's coded message was making Storm insist that we go to King Solomon's Mines before seeking out any other African treasure—I could just tell. I could also tell that Storm felt like she had to keep whatever it was a secret from the rest of us—even though it clearly hurt her to do it.

Hey, we're the Kidds. We don't hide things from one another.

Unless we have a very, very, *very* good reason.

Tommy rocked back in his chair and made a pained face. "Fine, but we're going to need a vehicle. Something major. A four-by-four that can handle sand and mud and elephant stampedes."

"We should contact Dumaka," said Storm.

"Who's he?" asked Beck.

"He was listed in Dad's phone book as his Cairo 'technology consultant.'"

"You actually memorized Dad's phone book?"

"Last December. I had some time to kill after Christmas."

"Wait a second," said Tommy. "If Dad had this Dumaka guy written down as his 'technology consultant,' Dumaka might do work for the CIA."

"So?"

"Well," said Beck, "if Dumaka knows we're in

Africa, it won't be too long before Uncle Timothy knows, too."

"Uncle Timothy already knows," said Storm. "Don't forget, he's one of Guy Dubonnet Merck's 'acquaintances.' Maybe it's time we gave Uncle T. a hint as to why we dropped out of school and where we're heading."

"Seriously?"

"Seriously."

I raised my hand. "This is all about that secret message you found hidden inside Mom's watch, right?"

"*Maybe.*"

From the way Storm said it, I could tell her "maybe" was secret code for "definitely."

CHAPTER 38

$\mathcal{A}$ nd then the weirdest thing happened: Storm
asked Beck and me to wait outside in the
street while she and Tommy had a "senior family
management" meeting inside the café.

"What's that supposed to mean?" demanded
Beck.

"Tommy and I need to discuss something that
I don't want you two to hear."

"Why not?"

"Yeah," I said. "We're a family. All for one
and one for all. We don't keep secrets from one
another."

Then Storm did something I swear I have never

seen her do before. She reached across the table with both hands to take one of Beck's, one of mine. "It's for your own protection, guys. I promise."

Wow. Now *she* was sounding and acting like *Mom*!

"We don't need protection," Beck fumed.

"Um, we might," I said.

"What?"

"Merck has a pistol, Beck." I pointed my finger and cocked back my thumb. "*Thwick, thwick.* Remember?"

"So?"

"He made Aunt Bela jump out a window."

"She had a jet pack!"

"Well, we don't."

Now Tommy raised his hand. "Um, could you guys take this one outside? Storm and I need to talk, I guess. In private."

None too happy about it, Beck and I did as we were told and went out to the street like a good little brother and sister.

We were pretty mad until a guy with a funny little monkey came along and did a few tricks for

a crowd of tourists. There's nothing like watching a dancing monkey juggling pistachio nuts and kicking strangers in the shins to help you forget how ticked off you are.

In fact, Beck and I were doubled over with laughter (the monkey had just crawled down a snooty, old English lady's blouse) when Tommy and Storm came out of the café.

"No more discussion, you guys," said Tommy. "We're going to King Solomon's Mines."

Now Tommy had that same pleading look in his eyes, too. They both clearly needed us to go along with whatever plan they just hatched.

So Beck and I decided to cut them a break.

"Fine," said Beck.

"Whatever," I added.

"We're treasure hunters," said Beck. "Let's go hunt some treasure."

"Awesome!" said Tommy, sounding totally relieved. "But first we need to find Dad's friend Dumaka. If we're going to drive thousands of miles across the burning desert and into the steaming jungle, we're going to need a serious set of wheels."

CHAPTER 39

D ad's friend Dumaka ran his clandestine operation in what was supposed to be a horizontal grain silo in an industrial zone of Cairo known as El Obour City.

He and his associates had about forty thousand square meters of open space to store all sorts of high-tech gear, including a couple of helicopters, several crates with EXPLOSIVES stenciled on them, and a specially equipped, totally tweaked-out Safari Extreme Global Expedition Vehicle.

It looked like the RV Darth Vader and his family would take on vacation.

"This expedition vehicle has been built in accordance with your father's exacting specifications," said Dumaka, a slight African man with a clipped British accent. He was wearing royal-blue coveralls and sported a neatly trimmed goatee. His eyes told me he was suspicious of everyone and everything in the cavernous warehouse, except maybe us.

"When did Dad give you these specs?" I asked, hoping his answer would prove that Dad was alive.

It didn't.

"Two, maybe three, years ago," said Dumaka. "There were several treasures he wished to recover in Africa. He requested that I customize a safari truck to rival your oceangoing vessel, *The Lost*. This off-road vehicle has several beds and a bathroom and shower, not to mention a fully equipped and stocked galley. It also has an in-motion satellite antenna system and a very sophisticated computer navigation system." Dumaka whispered what he said next: "There are also several secret compartments for you to hide valuables and items you do not wish falling into the wrong hands."

"What about power?" asked Tommy.

"Solar panels and diesel generator for electricity. Also, I built this four-by-four with a MaxxForce 15 engine instead of the standard 10."

"Is 15 good?" I asked. "Is there, like, a MaxxForce 20?"

Dumaka smiled. "Trust me, young Bick. This engine will give you the power of five hundred and fifty horses. While I do not recommend high speeds when off-roading, you can, if need be, fly faster than a herd of stampeding gazelles."

Dumaka stepped away for a moment and called out something to his work crew. *"Kila mtu, kuchukua dakika tano kazi mapumziko."*

Storm translated. "That's Swahili. He told everybody to take five."

As his workers shuffled off to a far corner of the stifling hot warehouse to drink cold beverages, Dumaka led us into the extreme Winnebago's main (and air-conditioned) cabin.

"The walls are thick and soundproof to protect us from prying eyes and curious ears. Now, children of my friend Dr. Thomas Kidd, we may speak freely."

CHAPTER 40

"**T**here are other features on this off-road vehicle I do not want my workers to know of," said Dumaka, his voice hushed.

"Are some of those guys out there spies?" I asked.

"Perhaps."

"Who are they working for?" asked Beck.

"That I cannot say. However, there is much chatter on back channels regarding several 'interested parties' who have recently arrived in Africa, all of them seeking treasure."

"Guy Dubonnet Merck?" I asked.

"So far, I have heard no names. However, if there is treasure to be plundered, Monsieur Merck will no doubt swoop in like a vulture to snatch it."

Just like he snatched the treasure map out of our hotel room near the pyramids.

Dumaka peeled back a corner of the dining room carpet to reveal the latch to one of the secret compartments.

"Under this hatch, you will find weapons and ammunition, should such armaments prove necessary. Up front, inside the driver's seat, you will find a secure satellite phone. The extraction package your father designed will go on full alert the moment you drive away. If and when you need us, simply call."

"Do you need access to our Swiss bank account?" asked Beck. "To pay for all this stuff?"

"Not to worry. Your father has already paid in full."

"Recently?" I asked, still eager for any confirmation that Dad was alive.

Dumaka shook his head. "Many years ago."

"How well did you know our father?" asked Tommy.

"Very well, indeed. Ten years ago, in Kinshasa,

Dr. Thomas Kidd saved my life as well as that of my brother, Nanji. Your father is a great man, and I would do a great many things for him. Now then, I trust one of you is old enough to drive?"

Tommy raised his hand. "I've got my international license, and I'm totally stoked to hit the road."

"Unfortunately, young Thomas Kidd," said Dumaka, "you will run out of roads before you reach your final destination. I have programmed the most direct route into the vehicle's secure and encrypted GPS. I have also input a few 'optional routes,' should you encounter any difficulties along the way."

"Excellent," said Tommy as he made his way up to the front to sit in the air-suspended command chair and fiddle with all of the vehicle's high-tech controls.

"Dumaka," said Storm, "if you don't mind, we need to do one more thing before we shove off."

"What is that?"

"Go back outside and drop a few bread crumbs."

CHAPTER 41

While Tommy messed with his knobs and played with the steering wheel, the rest of us followed Dumaka to the small break area, where his crew was still relaxing with cold bottled beverages.

"Thank you, Dumaka," Storm said loudly. "We're off to find King Solomon's Mines."

"Are you sure this is wise?" said Dumaka. "Some say the legendary diamond mines are just that: a legend. They say these mines do not actually exist."

"They do exist," said Storm. "And we know *exactly* where to find them."

"We have a treasure map," said Beck, playing along like we had agreed we would. "We'll be heading south. To Kukuanaland."

"Yes," I said. "Kukuanaland. For we know that the treasure lies in a cave just beyond the, uh…"

Beck jumped in. "The Suliman Berg Mountain Range. Remember?"

"Right. What she said."

Beck made a big show of gripping Dumaka's

hand. "So long, good friend. Thank you for equipping us with everything we need to, at long last, bring home the treasure of King Solomon's Mines!"

As the three of us walked back to the Safari Extreme Global Expedition Vehicle, Storm whispered, "Thanks, you guys."

"Um, did you notice the guy in the greasy watch cap?" I said, my voice hushed.

"Yeah."

"He was jotting down notes."

"Because he's a spy," said Beck.

"Probably, yes." said Storm.

"Uh, hello?" said Beck. "He's going to tell all those other treasure hunters exactly where we're going! He might even work for Merck!"

"I know," said Storm. "It's all part of the plan."

"The plan you and Tommy won't tell us about?"

"Yeah. That one."

"Fine," said Beck. "Like we said, we'll play along. But when this treasure quest is done, you and Tommy are gonna owe me and Bick big-time."

"We know," said Storm. "And so will Mom and Dad."

CHAPTER 42

Most of the lingering anger and resentment toward our older sibs was baked out of Beck and me by the time we were an hour outside Cairo.

Unrelenting desert sun and nothing to look at but miles and miles of sand, sand dunes, and sandy brush on both sides of the sand-swept road—which, by the way, is really just a narrow strip of sweltering black asphalt slicing through all that sand—will do that to you, even if you're traveling in a supercool, air-conditioned safari truck.

I guess sometimes you just have to trust your big brother and sister. Not too often. Just every now and then.

Okay, it's a long drive from Egypt to King Solomon's Mines, so here are some more history and geography facts for your reading pleasure. The Sahara is one of the world's hottest deserts. You could fry an egg on it if you didn't mind sand in your egg sandwiches.

It's also the second-largest desert in the world. Technically, Antarctica is the world's largest desert. Who knew? *Antarctica is a desert!* But, trust me, it's nowhere near as hot as the Sahara.

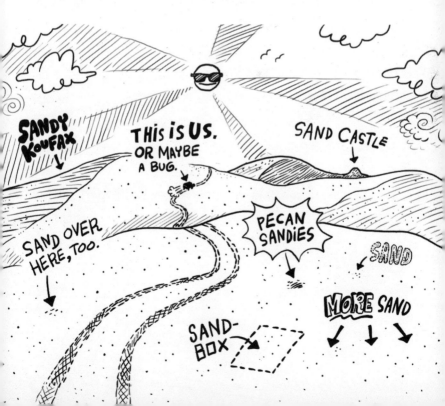

After miles of endless sand dunes (some as tall as 590 feet—about the height of the Space Needle in Seattle), we cruised through Luxor, the home of Hatshepsut's Temple, which is dedicated to the sun god Amon-Ra.

Farther down the road (we're talking hours and hours of sun and sand and license plate bingo, which is very hard to play when there aren't many cars on the road), we reached Aswan, where they have a big dam. And more sand.

Next we crossed the border into Sudan and the Nubian Desert.

THE GIANT SAND DUNES

ASWÂN DAM

TEMPLE OF LUXOR

I don't really know why they give these deserts names. They all kind of look the same. Although the Nubian one does seem to have more rocks and wadis, which I learned are dry riverbeds that only have water in them when it rains real hard. The rivers made a really bad call when they decided to flow through a *desert*.

Yes, all this desert stuff is actually pretty amazing and fascinating, and learning about it will no doubt make you a better person and help you get into Harvard or maybe even high school. This information is way more important to know than trivia like the names of the Egyptian gods, or, say, the names of all of Tommy's ex-girlfriends— which we got Storm to try to recite. (She got about halfway through before Tommy admitted he had no way of telling if she was right.)

But all was not fun and games.

When we were a few miles north of Khartoum, I decided to check out the expedition vehicle's superslick rearview periscope. It was a lot like those cameras some cars have in their rear ends that help you park without banging into people's bumpers, only this camera was up on a pole and could swivel.

I could see a shimmering wall of rippling heat waves rising up off the asphalt road behind us like in a mirage.

I also saw something else.

"Tommy? We have company," I said.

"Who?"

"Guy Dubonnet Merck."

CHAPTER 43

Tommy jammed the pedal to the metal.

Our super RV roared like a lion and took off. We were moving so fast our tires were kicking up a swirling sandstorm behind us.

But apparently Merck's jeeps and army trucks had souped-up engines, too—not to mention a lot less bulk and weight. Merck and his men emerged out of the angry brown dust cloud with their goggles down and their weapons up.

"He's going to shoot us!" I shouted, keeping my eye on that video periscope.

Bullets started pinging and bouncing off the back of our truck.

Good thing the design specs Dad gave to

Dumaka included armor plating and bulletproof glass.

"Initiating evasive maneuvers!" shouted Tommy as he started twisting the steering wheel left, then right, then left again. We weaved back and forth, lurching from side to side on the bumpy road. Tires squealed as Beck and I bounced against the galley walls and then tumbled into the living room sofa. The whole time it felt like we were on the verge of flipping over.

Using seat backs and countertops for handholds, Storm worked her way up to the cabin and plopped down in the passenger seat.

"Tommy?" she said.

"Yeah?"

"Take the next exit. Cross the river. Head into Khartoum."

Khartoum, of course, is the capital of Sudan. We took the Fitayhab Bridge into the city.

Merck was right behind us.

When we got into the city limits, Tommy's expert driving skills allowed us to finally lose the crazed Merck caravan in the crowded streets.

For, like, five minutes.

"They're baaaack," I announced from my perch with the periscope.

"We need an alternate route," said Storm, punching buttons on the sophisticated GPS.

A very pleasant female voice instructed us to *"Take the second left on Othman Digna Avenue."*

Tommy did as he was told.

Seconds later I saw Merck make the same turn.

"Turn right on Gamma Avenue, then left onto El Mek Nimir," said the GPS lady.

Tommy executed the right and the left. Merck did, too, and narrowed the gap.

"You guys?" said Beck, who was peering over

BAD GUYS MAY BE CLOSER THAN THEY APPEAR IN THE MIRROR.

my shoulder at the rearview video screen. "They're gaining on us."

"Where exactly is that GPS thing taking us?" I shouted.

A few more tire-screeching, hairpin turns and we were heading for the cargo terminals at Khartoum International Airport—and a fifteen-foot-tall chain-link fence topped with coiled concertina wire.

Tommy slammed on the brakes.

"Proceed to the guardhouse and wave at Samir," said the pleasant GPS voice. *"He is expecting you."*

Tommy eased the truck to a stop and waved at the scowling man with a machine gun inside the guard shack.

"You are Thomas Kidd?"

"Yes, sir."

"I am Samir. Please hurry. You do not wish to miss your flight to Zambia."

The gate slid open.

"In one hundred meters," cooed the GPS lady, *"drive into the cargo hold of the C-17 Globemaster military cargo aircraft."*

"What the…" was all Tommy said.

The instant we were inside the C-17, hydraulic arms raised the aircraft's tail ramp into its upright and locked position.

Cargo handlers in flight suits and helmets started working tie-down straps around our axles and bumpers, lashing us securely to the cargo hold's floor.

Someone tapped on the driver's side window.

Tommy lowered it.

"Welcome aboard, Kidds. I am Dumaka's brother, Nanji. If there is anything I can do to make your flight from Khartoum to Lusaka more comfortable, please do not hesitate to let me know. Now then, if you will please fasten your seat belts, we have been cleared for takeoff."

Talk about an amazing expedition vehicle.

It could fly like the wind on the open road.

Or, if you took the right alternate route, it could just fly!

CHAPTER 44

We figured we had a pretty good jump on Monsieur Merck when we landed in Zambia several hours later.

The roads between Khartoum and Lusaka are kind of sketchy, and there are very few rest stops or Holiday Inns along the way.

Then again, Merck might've hired a transport plane, too.

He might be only a few hours behind us.

"I wish you luck, brave children of Dr. Thomas Kidd," said Nanji as the rear cargo door lowered at the Lusaka airport.

"Thank you, Nanji," said Tommy as the two of them bumped fists. "We owe you, man!"

As we drove north, it was obvious that we weren't in the Sahara Desert anymore. The air was thick and steamy; the foliage lush and green. We were definitely in the tropics.

On the Great North Road between Lusaka and Kabwe, we passed a lot of small villages and police checkpoints. Misty green mountain peaks and towering white clouds lined the horizon. We saw giraffes for the first time, lapping water out of pools left by a passing rainstorm. We also saw a couple of monkeys and a zebra herd.

And then we saw our first pirates—of this trip anyway.

They were in a fast-moving Toyota pickup and started chasing after us on an empty stretch of road miles away from any of those handy police checkpoints. I counted six pirates crammed into the bed of the truck—all of them with bandoliers of bullets draped over their shoulders— ammunition for their Russian-made AK-47 machine guns. One pirate was toting a rocket-propelled grenade launcher.

"They look pretty fierce," said Beck, staring out the rear window. "A lot fiercer than Frenchy."

They were also faster.

The Toyota pulled alongside our expedition vehicle, which Tommy had pushed to do over a hundred miles an hour on the bumpy road.

One of the men threw a grappling hook onto the roof of our bucking truck, where it caught onto the satellite dish. The pirate with a machete gripped in his teeth swung over to board us.

225

"Bick?" Tommy shouted. "Take the wheel!"

"What?"

"Take the wheel. I'm going topside to deal with Captain Hook."

I jumped into the driver's seat the instant Tommy jumped out. Then I grabbed hold of the steering wheel and jammed my foot down on the accelerator. Fortunately, the road ahead was a straightaway, because this was basically my first driving lesson. The truck was rocking and rattling so much I thought my teeth might fly out of my head.

In the back, Storm had pulled back the carpet and was working open the hatch on the gun and ammunition compartment.

Tommy was standing on the control console between the two seats up front. He had popped open the moonroof and was reaching out to grab at the pirate's ankles.

I heard Tommy grunt.

Then I saw the bad guy slide down the windshield, smack our hood, tumble off to the road, and roll into a ditch.

"They're still chasing us!" Beck reported. "The Toyota pirates didn't stop to rescue their friend."

"They want our truck!" I said.

Tommy slid down from the moonroof and shut it tight.

"Well," he said, "they can't have it!"

CHAPTER 45

"**G**ive me back the wheel!" Tommy shouted. I slid out, and he slid in.

"Bick?" Beck called from the back. "Give me a hand. I have an idea."

Her lap was filled with boxes of Twinkies, Yodels, Ring Dings, and Sno Balls.

Our secret stash of junk food.

"Hurry," she said. "I can't carry it all."

"What's the plan?" I asked as I scooped up half the boxes.

"We open the rear window and toss them out. They go for the baked goods and leave us and the expedition vehicle alone."

"Hurry!" shouted Tommy from the driver's seat.

"I don't know how much longer this glorified Winnebago can keep up this kind of speed. Lug nuts are going to start popping off if I keep pushing it."

"Why can't we just shoot them?" asked Storm, who had discovered a double-barreled shotgun inside the secret weapons compartment.

"Because they have more and bigger guns," said Beck.

Tommy kept swerving our four-by-four back and forth across both lanes of the highway, forcing the pirates in the pickup to swerve behind our rear bumper.

Beck and I stumbled to the rear of the RV and flopped onto the foam mattress under the window, through which we could see the guy with the grenade launcher taking aim.

"Kick open the window!" Beck shouted. And in one fast motion, I did. "Toss 'em!"

We jettisoned all the boxes out the back.

A fruit pie splattered on the Toyota's windshield. Twinkies tumbled through the air. Plastic-wrapped cupcakes rolled down the road.

WHY IT'S IMPORTANT TO ALWAYS PACK SNACKS WHEN YOU GO ON A ROAD TRIP.

The driver slowed down because his comrades were banging on the roof of the pickup's cab, frantically pointing to the packages littering the highway.

The Toyota slammed on its brakes and squealed to a stop.

Five pirates jumped out the back and hurried off to collect their gooey goodies. Sweeter than gold! No one can resist a fully stocked Kidd snack stash.

Meanwhile, Tommy drove us off the highway and onto a rutted gravel road. Maybe a quarter mile down it, a huge herd of wildebeests—at least a mile long and four or five wildebeests thick—appeared out of nowhere, crossed the road, and basically created a massive moving roadblock behind us.

Tommy eased off the gas.

"Good work, you guys. The wildebeests will cover our tire tracks."

"Plus," said Beck, "it'll take them an hour to finish crossing. The pirates won't be able to chase after us, even if they want to."

"They may not want to," I said. "They looked pretty happy with the loot we threw at them."

"They should be," said Storm. "Sno Balls are hard to come by in Africa."

"Sorry about that," I said.

Storm shrugged. "At least you didn't give them our Oreos."

"We have Oreos?" said Beck. "You've been holding out on your dear little sis? Where are they?"

"Ha! I'll never tell."

We all laughed a little.

The way you do when you realize you could've lost something much more important than cookies or cupcakes.

We could've lost our lives.

CHAPTER 46

Tommy drove us deeper into the Zambian jungle. I could see elephants plodding beneath ropey-trunked trees. A leopard slunk through the underbrush in search of some food. It was like we were in a zoo but without any cages.

"They'll be back," I mumbled about an hour after we'd lost the pirates. Beck nodded. "If not them, somebody else."

"That's why we need to ditch this vehicle," said Tommy. "It's not exactly inconspicuous. We're going to have to finish our trip to King Solomon's Mines on foot."

CHAPTER 47

Miles into the unbelievably humid jungle—
after we forded a stream where the water
rose up to our RV's door handles—we came upon
a small village.

The people living there were extremely friendly,
so, after some back and forth, we stashed our
Safari Extreme Global Expedition Vehicle in a
large thatched hut (after paying the owner hand-
somely for long-term parking privileges) and made
our way to a very convenient Rent-A-Guide stand,
where we tried to hire a safari team to take us

farther into the jungle, up into Kukuanaland and on to King Solomon's Mines.

That wasn't so easy, actually.

The guides and porters, including a man named Sonkwe, who ran the hut, basically laughed in our faces.

"We will not take orders from disheveled children," said Sonkwe. "That is a surefire recipe for disaster and possibly death."

"What if we gave you a ton of money?" said Tommy.

"How much?"

"Five hundred dollars?"

The men all laughed.

"Tommy?" said Beck. "Step aside." And the Kidd family's chief negotiator took over.

Meanwhile, Tommy drifted off to explore the rest of the village.

There were some very pretty girls about his age, all of them dressed in matching skirts, bikini tops, and brightly colored head wraps, practicing some awesome dance moves over in a clearing

THE LOCALS NEGOTIATED WITH ME—
INSOFAR AS ONE CAN NEGOTIATE WITH ONE'S BACK
TURNED WHILE PLAYING A GAME OF DICE IN THE DIRT.

where some guys were whaling on big, oblong drums. Of course, Tommy got distracted and was no help at all.

After about twenty minutes of haggling, Beck sealed the deal at the Rent-A-Guide hut. Sonkwe and six others would lead us through the jungle and up into the mountains for less than Tommy offered but with a 15 percent royalty on everything we found inside King Solomon's Mines, "which might be worth millions," according to Beck.

"This is a very fair deal," said Sonkwe when he and Beck shook on it. "We shall leave first thing tomorrow morning."

Storm, Beck, and I hurried off to tell Tommy the good news.

He was still with the dancers, taking a turn on one of the drums. He had, of course, made "friends" with a beautiful local girl who didn't speak a word of English.

Apparently, our crude sign language worked. The girl looked terrified.

As she ran away, she surprised us by shriek-ing the two English words she apparently knew: "Marry me! Marry me! Marry me!"

"I guess I taught her that," Tommy said with an embarrassed chuckle.

"Thomas?" said Storm, using her best stern voice. "Did you ask that girl to marry you?"

"Duh. Several times. I'm in love, you guys.

I swear. No funny business. This time I am so totally serious. That girl's going to be Mrs. Tailspin Tommy!"

"What's her name?"

"Oops," he said, grinning sheepishly. "Forgot to ask."

CHAPTER 48

Sonkwe and his team led us deep into the jungle.

"We must hurry," he said. "If, as you say, you angered the pirates who rule the Great North Road, they will surely seek revenge. And soon."

We threw our gear together double-quick.

One of our guides was a very bizarre, elderly British gentleman with snow-white hair and a neatly trimmed goatee. He was decked out in a pith helmet, safari shirt, khaki shorts, and knee-socks like a Great White Hunter from an old Tarzan movie.

He also had an odd way of introducing himself. "Chip, chip, cheerio. I'm Fred. Lord Fred. Formerly with MI-Five. British Intelligence, what-what?"

"You were a spy?" said Beck.

"I prefer the term *bird-watcher.*"

"So how'd you end up in *this* line of work?" asked Tommy, who's always interested in everybody's life story. "Carrying heavy stuff on your back in the steamy jungles of Africa?"

"Hard work and dedication, old bean. Now it's all tickety-boo."

We followed Lord Fred, Sonkwe, and the others up a narrow, vine-choked path. The guides in the lead slashed at the tangled green creepers with their machetes.

LORD FRED

HE'S A BRIT AND A BIT OF A TWIT.

WHAT-WHAT?

It was jungle, jungle everywhere. Nothing but jungle. Hot, humid, sticky, sweaty, forehead-dribbling, shirt-soaking, back-trickling JUNGLE.

To make things worse, Storm decided to regale us with her encyclopedic knowledge of everything that might be lurking in the dewy green darkness all around us.

Most of it, apparently, was poisonous. Poisonous plants, poisonous bugs, poisonous snakes, even poisonous tree frogs and fire ants.

Have you ever read the epic Greek adventure tale *The Odyssey*? Well, Mom made us read that and *The Iliad*. *The Odyssey* is about this guy on a really long trip to get home to his family, but it takes him, like, twenty years. This trip was starting to feel a lot like that, except happening to us instead of an old Greek guy.

The dangers we had to deal with in the African jungle were very, very real, and they could make us very, very dead.

But once you decide something in a family meeting (like making a run at King Solomon's Mines), there's really no turning back.

Especially when you know a band of snack-cake-crazed-sugar-buzzed pirates is following you.

CHAPTER 49

We came to a swiftly flowing river churning with white-water rapids.

"We must cross here," said Sonkwe. "Inflate the rubber rafts. Load up the gear. Kidd children? You will split up and take separate rafts, each with one of my guides, for your protection."

Tommy and Storm climbed into their own raft with Sonkwe. Beck and I were assigned the raft piloted by Lord Fred.

Of course, neither of us trusted Lord Fred as far as we could throw a bull elephant—if, you know, we could even *lift* a bull elephant. Maybe it was his teensy-tiny, beady eyes. Or his Kentucky Fried Chicken—dude beard and mustache. Could've been that none of the other guides wore kneesocks or pith helmets or said "chip, chip, cheerio" like the chimney sweeps in *Mary Poppins*.

But, most likely, Beck and I didn't trust Lord Fred because he told us he used to be a spy.

A lot of spies (our own parents not included) are supershady, and you never know whose side they're really on. They could be double agents or triple agents, and I'm pretty sure I heard once about a quadruple agent. They could trick you into thinking they were working for you when, in fact, they were working for your worst enemy while simultaneously working for *that* enemy's enemy.

Did Lord Fred work for Guy Dubonnet Merck? Even worse, was Nathan Collier, our parents' number one competitor, Fred's real boss? Did Fred know Uncle Timothy or Aunt Bela?

"Right-oh, children," said Fred. "Time to shove off, what-what?"

It was a hot and sweltering day (one hundred degrees with 100 percent humidity), so I was actually looking forward to crossing the roaring river. I was hoping there might be some kind of cooling breeze wafting across the rapids, maybe a refreshing spray from the choppy water. I figured the river would be a nice break from hiking through the sticky, steamy jungle.

I was so wrong.

THEY CALL THEM RAPIDS 'CAUSE THEY DROWN YOU REALLY FAST.

CHAPTER 50

Our raft (and for some reason—most likely Lord Fred—just our raft) was swept downstream by the river's unrelenting current.

We shot down the rapids, cascaded over a waterfall, landed with a hard splash, and found ourselves drifting across the glassy surface of a wide lake.

"Where's everybody else?" shouted Beck.

"Back upstream," I said. "Crossing the river. Like *we* were supposed to do!"

Then we glared at our so-called guide, Lord Fred.

"Right-oh," he said. "Keep calm and carry on. No need to panic. I believe this is Lake Bangweshiba.

Should be smooth sailing from here on out."

"Smooth sailing?" Beck shouted. "Lake Bang-whatever isn't where we're supposed to be! It's not even on Storm's treasure map!"

"We need to be on the other side of that river with the others," I added.

"We sure do," said Beck. "Because we didn't pack any food or gear on this raft! The porters took it all in *their* rafts."

"Right," said Lord Fred. "You children raise some very interesting and valid points. Let me think about all of it for a tick, what-what?"

While Fred thought, we kept drifting.

On the horizon, behind an island with two jagged peaks, the sun was starting to set, cooling the air and turning the sky a gorgeous, *Lion King* orange.

We might have been lost and cut off from our family, but, for the moment, everything was extremely peaceful.

Until about two seconds later.

CHAPTER 51

At this point in the story, I would like to quote my sister Beck: "OMG!"

A giant hippo rose up out of the lake, showing nothing but jaws and teeth. We're talking an enormous and deadly mouth stretching open no more than five feet away from our dinky, little rubber raft.

As the huge thing blew water out of its snout like wet snot, I was remembering all the fun factoids Storm had shared with us about *hippopotami*, which is Latin for "hippopotamuses."

The blubbery, nearly hairless beast keeps cool by staying submerged all day long and comes out at night only to munch on grass—or any children it might find floating across its lake on a rubber raft. The hippo is also one of the heaviest land mammals in the world (right behind elephants and some rhinos), but, despite its stocky body and stubby legs, this hippo could easily outrun Beck and me. Imagine a two-ton tank with jaws of death tearing after you at twenty miles per hour, and you've got a pretty good picture of a hippo.

Storm had also been kind enough to mention that "the hippopotamus is one of the most aggressive creatures on earth and one of the most dangerous animals in all of Africa." Storm had also shared the facts that hippopotamus teeth sharpen themselves as they grind together and that their lower canines can grow to be twenty inches long!

Good to know. Especially when you're staring down the wide-open mouth of one. I'd hate to be this guy's dentist. If you think morning breath is bad, you should get a whiff of hippo mouth.

But the hippo didn't bite us with his jumbo-sized choppers.

Oh, no. It did something much worse.

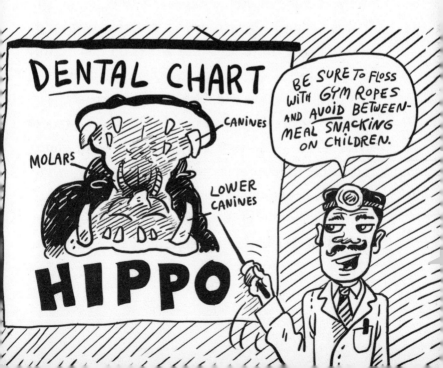

CHAPTER 52

It flipped the raft!

It dipped its ginormous head under our raft and pitched us over like half-baked pancakes.

Beck and I tumbled into the water.

I was thinking piranhas. I was thinking crocodiles. I was thinking water snakes! I was thinking about that hippo with the enormous teeth.

And leeches over 99.9 percent of my body.

Yes, thrashing around in the mud-swirled waters, all I could think about were all those incredibly hideous, poisonous, and predatory creatures Storm had warned us about.

I reached out blindly with both hands, hoping to find Beck, but slightly worried that I might be

sticking my arms down the raft-tossing hippo's throat. Fortunately, my fingers locked onto Beck's and, even though we couldn't see each other, we scissor-kicked our way to the surface.

When we broke through the water and gasped for breath, the hippopotamus was gone.

So was Lord Fred.

"You think the hippo got him?" said Beck.

"Maybe," I replied. "Could've been a crocodile, though. Or a piranha. Might've been a poisonous water snake."

"So Lord Fred is, basically, dead?"

We were both treading water, keeping our eyes out for any slow-moving logs with eyeballs— better known as crocodiles. I kicked off my shoes because I swim better barefoot.

"I guess there's a chance Fred escaped," I said. "After all, he told us he used to be a spy. Maybe he remembered some of his MI-Five survival skills."

"Well, what about us?" demanded Beck. "He's our guide! He just leaves us stranded in the middle of a lake with a ruptured rubber raft?"

A sheet of limp plastic drifted by like a deflated pool float after someone attacked it with a pitch-fork.

"Maybe you can demand a refund from Sonkwe," I suggested.

"Don't worry. I will!"

"Meanwhile," I said, "why don't we swim to that island."

"That's not an island, Bickford. That's two pointy rocks with a sad little tree."

"Without any hippos on them," I said. "Or piranhas, or leeches, or..."

"Fine. You win."

And so we swam. Fast.

After living most of our lives on the ocean, Beck and I are both excellent swimmers. We soared across that lake like we were riding Jet Skis. We might've beaten the Olympic record for the 100-meter freestyle. Of course, the crocodile that started chasing after us probably had something to do with our record-breaking speed. Crocodiles tend to be great motivators.

We made it to the double rocks.

And, for the first time, after all those years of being at sea, the two of us were actually stranded on a desert island...*in the middle of the jungle.*

CHAPTER 53

It gets very dark at night in the jungle. There's zero glow from bright city lights to dim the diamond-studded African sky.

As Beck and I huddled against our solitary tree on the rocks, I wished I had my Dad's rain slicker with me. The night air was actually chilly.

I shivered a little and Beck's teeth chattered.

And then we heard the swish of crocodile tails circling our "island." And hippos blowing water out of their noses. And snakes slithering across the lake. I could also hear a big cat grum-bling somewhere off in the distance. Perfect.

"Um, Beck?"

"Yeah?"

"I know house cats don't like water, but can African lions swim?"

"Probably," said Beck. "Depends on how hun-gry they are."

"How about cheetahs?"

"They'll swim if they're chasing their dinner."

"What about leopards? Do they swim, too?"

"Sure. Especially if they want to get dinner before the lions and cheetahs eat it all. Satisfied, Bick?"

"Yeah. Thanks."

And then neither of us said another word for about an hour. Yes, we were breaking all sorts of world records.

But then, suddenly, Beck stood up.

"Did you hear that?"

"What?" I said.

"Shhh! Listen."

"All I hear is my heart beating and the crocodiles discussing what they're going to have for dinner if the big cats eat us first!"

"Shhh. Seriously. I think I hear someone calling our names."

I strained to listen.

Then I heard it, too. Way off in the distance, a faint chorus of "Bick? Beck? Rebecca? Bickford? Where are you, old chaps?" came through the darkness.

It was Tommy, Sonkwe, and Lord Fred.

"You guys!" I shouted. "We're out here!"

"Tommy?" Beck screamed. "We're on these stupid little rocks!"

We kept it up for five full minutes. But no one shouted back. Our rescue party had moved on.

"This is all Fred's fault," said Beck, sitting down with a huff. "I hate him."

"Yeah?" I said. "Well, I hate him more."

And, believe it or not, stranded on our tiny desert island, we launched into Twin Tirade No. 470.

"Impossible, Bickford. I hate Lord Fred more than brussels sprouts smeared with moldy mayonnaise."

"Oh really, Rebecca? Well, I don't just hate Lord Fred, I *loathe* him. I abhor, detest, and despise him! He is an anathema and abomination!"

"What? What does that mean?"

"That I hate him more than you!"

That was when a big, noisy bird landed on one of the rocks. Beck and I suspended our tirade and scurried over to the other rock to let our nasty wing-flapping visitor have its pick of the peaks.

At least we thought it was a big bird. It was so dark we couldn't actually see what had just landed on our rock cluster. But we could definitely hear it. The thing was a real squawker, like the pterodactyls in all the movies.

Maybe it *was* a pterodactyl.

Beck and I wouldn't know for sure until first thing in the morning.

If we lived that long.

CHAPTER 54

I t was probably the scariest, longest night of our entire lives.

The sound effects alone would've driven most kids (or adults) crazy. We're talking bird squawks, hippo snorts, hyena laughs, snake hisses, and man-eating lion roars. I could also, I swear, hear the bloodsucking leeches puckering up their blood suckers.

To make matters worse, I also heard Storm's nonstop "The Horrors of the Jungle" mono-logue floating through my brain in an endless audio loop: "Think about this, you guys: A Nile crocodile named Gustave, on the other side of Lake Tanganyika, is twenty-one feet long and weighs two thousand pounds.

"Crocodiles are like goldfish. They don't stop growing as long as they have a steady flow of food. Well, Gustave is so huge he can't get by on a diet of fish and antelope meat like all the other crocodiles. Oh, no. Now, he attacks larger animals. Hippopotamuses, wildebeests, and even humans!"

The memory made me gulp.

NOW I KNOW HOW CAPTAIN HOOK FELT!

"At least we're not stranded in South America," mumbled Beck somewhere off in the darkness.

"What?" I said.

"I was remembering all that scary stuff Storm told us about Gustave, the Nile crocodile."

"Me too!"

(We're twins. What can I say? Sometimes we even share the same nightmares.)

"But," said Beck, "Gustave is only *one* freakishly large African croc. The black caiman crocodiles that live in the Amazon basin of South America are much worse."

"Worse than a psycho killer who cuts through whole crowds of people just so he can chomp a bite out of every butt he bumps into?"

"Lots worse. The black caiman crocodiles have no natural predator, Bick. Do you know what that means?

"They're at the tippy-top of the food chain?"

"That's right. If the black caimans swam across the ocean to Africa, they'd be the real kings of the jungle. Nothing can stop a black caiman!"

I thought about that.

"What about a Black Hawk?" I said.

"Huh?"

"I bet a Black Hawk helicopter could beat a black caiman crocodile."

And—in the middle of the lake in the middle of the night—we started Twin Tirade No. 471.

"No way, Bickford. The black caiman would clamp its jaws on the Black Hawk's landing gear and drag it underwater."

BLACK CAIMAN CROC VS. BLACK HAWK HELICOPTER

- SCALY BLACK SKIN, PERFECT CAMOUFLAGE FOR NIGHT ATTACKS

- LARGEST PREDATOR IN AMAZON BASIN

- SOMETIMES EATS PEOPLE

- ONLY **2,000** LEFT IN THE WORLD AND THEY KNOW WHO TO BLAME FOR THAT— US!

- CAN LIVE TO BE **80** YEARS OLD

- FOUR BLADES, TWIN ENGINES

- MAX SPEED OF 193 MILES PER HOUR

- ARMORED!

- CAN CARRY 11 COMBAT-EQUIPPED TROOPS

- RANGE OF **320** NAUTICAL MILES

- EATS ONLY OIL AND GASOLINE

"Only if the chopper pilot was dumb enough to drop down that low!"

"The black caiman croc can grow sixteen, twenty feet long!" said Beck. "It would jump out of the water and clamp its high-pressure jaws on your helicopter—"

"And get a Hellfire laser-guided missile down its snout."

"Which the croc would just chomp in half."

"So I'd shoot it with my side-mounted Gatling guns."

We leaned against each other.

"The bullets would bounce off the crocodile's dinosaur-thick hide."

I yawned first. "Not if they were armor-piercing bullets."

"The croc would just...frumple miffenshish..." mumbled Beck.

"Moonka hinka miffenpish fooph," I mumbled back.

And then, totally exhausted, holding on to each other for dear life, we both drifted off to sleep.

We never finished our tirade.

CHAPTER 55

The sun peeked up over the eastern edge of the lake.

"Mom and Dad?" I mumbled groggily. "Are we at King Solomon's Mines yet?"

"Are we there yet?" mumbled Beck.

Yeah, sometimes we have the same wake-up dreams, too.

That was the good news: We actually woke up. Big Bird had flown the coop—though I did see a suspiciously large egg perched on the peak where it had roosted.

But it was a new dawn.

Somehow, Beck and I had lived to see another glorious day.

We also lived to see another raft.

At first, it was just a black blob against the rising sun.

Then it was definitely a raft. Then it became two rafts. Three!

"Woo-hoo!" shouted Beck, waving her arms above her head. "Over here!"

I joined in. "You guys? Hurry! Before birdo-saurus comes back!"

Tailspin Tommy was in the lead raft. Storm was in the one right behind him. That hippo that dunked Beck and me? It rose up and worked open its enormous mouth to roar at Storm.

Storm roared back.

Storm's roar was scarier.

"And brush your teeth!" Storm shouted when the terrified hippo dived under the water for protection. "All four of them!"

Guess who was in the third raft? None other than that lily-livered coward Lord Fred. When he and Tommy scurried up the rocks to rescue us, Lord Fred acted like he was the best friend Beck and I ever had.

"I was frightfully worried about you two last night. Thought I might never sleep again. Fortunately, I did. Spot of warm milk and a good book and I was out like a light. How about you two? Everything tickety-boo?"

That was when Beck kneed him. Right in his "tickety-boo," where it really, really hurts. Lord Fred groaned.

But I was the one who screamed. "What the…? Why are my feet green?"

CHAPTER 56

Maybe it was because I had spent the night worrying about reptiles and amphibious creatures but suddenly my feet looked like they belonged on Kermit the Frog. They hadn't turned into flippers, but they were definitely green.

"They tingle and itch," I said. "My feet are all prickly...."

"And how gross is this," said Beck, studying my feet. "There's a ton more dead skin flaking off between your toes than usual."

Not that anybody asked her, but that was when

Storm decided to join us to offer her Unlicensed Medical Genius opinion.

"I suspect," she said, without any hint of emotion, "that our unfortunate brother has trench foot, a condition caused by prolonged exposure of the feet to damp, unsanitary, and cold conditions."

"We're in the jungle!" shouted Beck. "How could Bick's feet get cold?"

"They did," I admitted. "Last night. After the sun went down."

"Oh, my," said Lord Fred. "This is a bit of a sticky wicket. I best radio the base camp to let them know of our predicament, what-what?"

Lord Fred scampered down the rocky slope, climbed onto his raft, and started working his walkie-talkie.

Meanwhile, Storm, Beck, and Tommy moved in to make a tight family circle around me.

"What can we do?" asked Tommy.

Storm shook her head. "Not much from here. If left untreated—which we'll have to do, at least for a while, since we are nowhere near a hospital or even a walk-in clinic—trench foot usually results in a painful case of gangrene. That leads to a painful amputation and then, given our current jungle environment and the high probability of reinfection...well, it won't be good."

"W-w-*whoa*," I stammered. "Back up a little.

P-p-painful gangrene? P-p-painful amputation?
What comes after that?!"

"*Painful* death, little brother." Storm dropped
the bomb of truth like only she knows how. "With
our current amount of resources and lack of medical expertise, it's almost certain. But be brave.
We'll tell Mom that you sacrificed yourself so the
rest of us could save her."

CHAPTER 57

S o there I was, staring at my green feet and my very certain death, when Beck and I launched into Twin Tirade No. 472.

We both knew it might be one of our last.

So we made it a good one, maybe our best ever.

"You know what I hate most about dying?" I said to Beck. "Losing you."

"Hang on. I'm going to miss you more than you'll miss me."

"Impossible."

"What do you mean? You won't even be here, Bickford. How can you miss anything in this world if you're not in it anymore?"

"Wherever I am, I'll miss you, Rebecca! More than you'll ever know."

"Impossible. Because I love you more than you'll ever know."

"Wrong again. I know *exactly* how much you love me because I know how much I love you."

Beck stretched out her arms. "I'm talking about a love this big, Bickford. There's no way you love me more than this!"

"Really? Well, my love for you is bigger than that hippo that capsized us yesterday."

"So? My love for you is bigger than that same hippo inside a black caiman's belly after the jumbo crocodile eats it."

Tailspin Tommy whistled. "That's big, Bick."

Storm agreed. "Humongous."

We were done with the tirade. It was time for a hug. We fell into each other's arms the same way we fell into them the night before.

"Give me some of that!" said Tommy, moving in to join us.

"Make room for me," said Storm, sniffling back a tear. I figured her emotions had finally caught up with her. We all clung to one another in a rugby scrum of a family hug. There wasn't a dry eye in the clump.

"Mind if I join in, chaps?" called Lord Fred from his rubber raft.

"Yes!!!" we all shouted at the same time.

We didn't want anyone to ruin our final hug as a family.

CHAPTER 58

L ord Fred joined us on our rock.

"Righty-oh, then," he said. "After young Master Bickford shuffles off this mortal coil, we press on, what-what?"

"What?!" said Beck.

"I'm simply suggesting that once your brother dies, the rest of us should continue on our quest to find King Solomon's Mines—after giving the poor chap a proper burial, of course. Maybe one of those Viking funerals with a burning boat here on the lake, what-what? Of course, we don't want to waste too much time on the funeral. Those pirates chasing after us have undoubtedly gained a good deal of ground during this brief and unfortunate detour...."

"I'm ignoring you," said Beck. "This is the darkest day of my life."

"Not to worry," said Lord Fred. "The sun should burn through those clouds any minute now."

"Yo, Fred?" said Tommy.

"Yes, Master Thomas?"

"Stick a sock in it."

"Yeah," said Storm. "Or I'll knee you in your tickety-boo like Beck did."

"Righty-oh, then," said Lord Fred, snapping a crisp salute off the brim of his pith helmet. "I will be in my raft awaiting further instructions."

He slipped onto his rubber raft and started fiddling with a yellow box that looked like an old-fashioned transistor radio.

Beck knelt beside me on the rock. I almost couldn't believe how sad she was.

But then I remembered our last adventure, when Beck had been the one in serious trouble.

She had been kidnapped by Nathan Collier's thugs. When I thought we had lost her for good, it was as if someone had split me in half. See, twins sometimes feel each other's pains and emotions, even when they're miles apart. Well, I know Beck and I do.

We've always been together, even before we were born.

Will that end when one of us dies? Will something special inside the twin who's left behind die, too?

Yep. Things were getting pretty bleak on the rock. Dark clouds of doom were hovering over our heads.

Then things got even darker.

Seriously. Something was blocking out the sun and casting a huge shadow over our "island." And it wasn't a cloud—it was a helicopter. Not a Black Hawk. Something even stealthier. In fact, I was pretty sure it was a CIA spy chopper.

Because strange Uncle Timothy was riding in the passenger seat.

CHAPTER 59

"Good work on the landing beacon, Frederick," Uncle Timothy said after he had climbed out of his high-tech helicopter.

That yellow box with the antenna Fred had been fiddling with? He must have used it to send up a signal to guide in Uncle Timothy's chopper. The perfectly balanced whirlybird teetered on the tip of one of the two pointy peaks.

Uncle Timothy touched the Bluetooth device jammed in his left ear. "Major Lin? Fly the bird to the LZ. I'll babysit the packages and water evac them to safety. Keep your ears on the Music Box for COMINT and sanitize our flight plans. *Zàijiàn.*"

Beck and I looked at each other and shrugged our shoulders. When Uncle Timothy started spewing spy lingo, none of us ever knew what he was talking about.

The helicopter lifted off, zoomed across the lake, and shot out over the surrounding jungle.

Uncle Timothy, of course, was wearing his mirrored sunglasses (he even wears them to sleep), so I couldn't read his eyes. But I had a feeling he expected the four of us to start grilling him with questions about why he was following us.

Instead, I said, "What's going on with my mom and dad? I want the truth, Uncle Timothy. If I'm going to die, I want to know if they're still alive. Call it my dying request."

"Yeah," echoed Beck. "What exactly is happening with Mom right now? And where is Dad?"

Uncle Timothy tapped his Bluetooth earpiece. "Turkey Trot Two? Initiate your sonar scans. Chart your magnetometer, metal detector, and ROV hits. I'll join you later. Right now, I have to deal with blowback on a family dynamic."

Apparently, my green feet and bothersome

questions were keeping Uncle Timothy from some very important clandestine operation.

"You want the truth?" he said.

For a second I didn't know if he was talking to me or Turkey Trot Two in his earpiece.

"Yes," I said. "I want an honest answer!"

"Well, son, I honestly don't know. Either that or I honestly won't tell you. However, I did bring medical supplies."

He unzipped a pouch on his safari vest. First, he pulled out a pair of dry socks and a packet of toe warmers. "Warm your feet for five minutes. Keep them dry. Rotate fresh socks on a regular basis. Try not to sweat so much."

"Good luck with that, what-what?" said Lord Fred, whose forehead was spritzing like a lawn sprinkler.

Next, Uncle Timothy pulled out a syringe loaded with medicine.

"Broad-spectrum antibiotics," said Uncle Timothy, flicking the syringe with his finger to dislodge an air bubble. "Should help. You're not going to die, Bick. At least not today."

Beck and I exhaled with relief. "Thank you!"

"You may lose a foot or two, but you'll live. Guess you won't be able to play soccer for Chumley Prep when I ship you back to New York—which, by the way, I plan to do just as soon as you can hobble home!"

CHAPTER 60

Tommy hoisted me in his arms and carried me down to one of the rubber rafts.

"Keep your feet up, Bick!" he said as he waded into the water. "You heard Uncle T. You need to keep 'em dry."

"And," said Beck, "you need to wear clean socks on a regular basis, not just sniff-test your dirty ones to pick a pair. I know personal hygiene is a novel concept for you, but, seriously, Bick, you need to kick it up a notch."

When we arrived at the camp Sonkwe had set up on the far side of the raging river, Tommy carried me to a cot in a tent and draped Dad's yellow rain slicker on top of my blanket.

"That'll help you feel better," he said with a wink.

After I was settled in my bed, the whole family gathered around to pray, the way we used to every night with Mom and Dad. Well, everybody except Storm. She abstained.

"I have my own way of communicating with the higher power."

She sat cross-legged on the floor of the tent and chanted "ohm" a lot.

Uncle Timothy also abstained from the family prayer, as did his pilot, Major Lin. But Uncle Timothy did serenade me with some very nice guitar strumming. I guess he always takes a six-string on his top secret spy missions. Anyway, he was playing and singing the opening track from the Beach Boys' *Pet Sounds* album while Major Lin kept the beat on an empty water bottle.

"Wouldn't it be nice if we were older…"

Storm snapped out of her meditation.

"'Wouldn't it be nice if we were older'? Is that supposed to be a dig?"

Uncle Timothy stopped singing.

"I beg your pardon?"

Major Lin was confused, too. "*Wǒ bù míngbái*," he said as he stopped bopping his bottle.

"Just because we're younger than you," said Storm defensively, "doesn't mean we can't handle ourselves."

Uncle Timothy sniggered. "Young Bickford's lime-green feet seem to suggest otherwise, Stephanie."

Major Lin chuckled.

Storm was about to turn into Thunder Storm. She didn't like it when anybody called her by her real name, except, of course, Mom and Dad.

Uncle Timothy was neither.

CHAPTER 61

Storm was about to go Incredible-Hulk-ballistic on Uncle Timothy when Tommy held up his hand to let her know he'd handle it.

"Back off, Uncle Timothy," he said. "You're totally out of line."

"Yeah," I said from my sickbed. "We know what we're doing."

"And why were you following us, anyway?" demanded Beck.

"I wasn't 'following' you, Rebecca," said Uncle Timothy. "I have pressing business of my own here in Africa. You see, children, when I received the distress signal from Frederick—"

"He works for you, doesn't he?" I said, propping myself up in bed. "He's a spy's spy!"

"I prefer to think of him as a chaperone. Someone to babysit you children while you work on your Jungle Survivorship merit badges."

"Well," said Storm, "you can tell our 'chaperone' that as soon as Bick is able to hike again, we'll be continuing our quest to find King Solomon's Mines."

"So I have heard," said Uncle Timothy.

"Oh, really? Where?"

"I have eyes and ears everywhere, children. However, I must admit I was a bit surprised by your choice of treasure. I know it's on your father's to-do list, but so are many others."

"Dad left us a very detailed map," blurted Beck. "So we know exactly where to find the mines."

That was when strange Uncle Timothy did something I have never seen him do before. He whipped off his sunglasses so he could squint at Storm like a gunslinger.

"Did your father leave you any other maps, Stephanie?"

NOTE HOW NEITHER ONE **EVER** BLINKS.

"Nope," said Storm. Because she's so unemotional, she's the best liar in the family. "Just the one."

"You're not lying to me, are you?"

Storm and strange Uncle Timothy stared at each other for what seemed like hours.

"I'm not lying," Storm finally said. "We're children. We don't know how to lie the way adults do."

Uncle Timothy grinned and buffed his mirrored shades on the tail of his safari shirt. Major

Lin suddenly piped up: "They could be lying about their final destination."

"Impossible," said Uncle Timothy.

"How can you be so sure?" said Lin.

"Look at young Bick's feet. Would these children have endured all that they have if their eyes weren't firmly fixed on a prize they believe is waiting for them just over the next mountain ridge?"

Major Lin shook his head. "No. Not unless they were complete idiots."

"Which we're totally not, dude," said Tommy. "So, you know, deal with it."

Uncle Timothy stood up.

"I wish you good luck in your quest."

And then he dropped his latest bombshell.

"However…"

"What?" said Tommy.

"I'm not trying to scare you—well, actually, I am—but I must tell you something."

"So tell us!" snapped Beck.

"I'm not the only one following you."

CHAPTER 62

"We know," said Beck. "Those Zambian pirates we pelted with Twinkies on the Great North Road have been tailing us for days."

"They are not alone," said Uncle Timothy with a sly smile. "In fact, they have joined forces with Guy Dubonnet Merck, whom I believe you've met.

"And Merck and the Zambian pirates aren't the only fiends you children need to fear. Intelligence indicates that Nathan Collier is also headed to Africa."

"Wow," said Tommy, sounding impressed. "You sure have to keep tabs on a ton of people, Uncle Timothy."

"Comes with the territory, Thomas."

And that was when I drifted off. The antibiotics were working. My fever was starting to break, but I was totally zonked. I drifted off to dreamland.

When I woke up, it was dark out again. Beck told me I'd been muttering in my sleep.

"You kept saying 'thirteen' and 'Caesar' over and over." She was whispering because weird Uncle Timothy was still lurking outside the tent.

"I had the strangest dream," I told her. "Thirteen Julius Caesars had thirteen seizures after eating thirteen rancid Caesar salads."

"You're still trying to figure out that thing Mom said, huh?"

"Yeah, I guess."

"Don't worry. I think Storm already has and—"

That was when Uncle Timothy burst into the tent. Tommy and Storm were right behind him.

"I think you children need to reconsider your plans here in Africa," Uncle Timothy said. "Our chief of station in Kenya has informed me that the nefarious Nathan Collier just docked his submarine at the port city of Mombasa. That's only a five-hour flight from here."

"I told you," said Tommy, "we're not afraid of Collier."

"Just that gunk he gels his hair with," said Beck.

Beck's crack made me laugh. It made Uncle Timothy mad.

"Look, you two small children and you two small-minded older children: None of you has any business out here in the jungle."

"Except for, you know, all the treasure in King Solomon's Mines," said Tommy.

"That's our family business," added Beck. "Treasure hunting!"

"Well, one day," fumed Uncle Timothy, "on one of these ridiculous treasure hunts, you will all die, and I will write the blockbuster, bestselling, tell-all book about your grisly deaths and cash in, big-time!"

I was feeling better, so I sat up in my cot.

"And one day, you'll die, too, fake Uncle Timothy. Speaking of which—are Mom and Dad still alive?"

Uncle Timothy scowled at me.

"I'm sorry, Bickford. That information is classified."

CHAPTER 63

The next morning, I was feeling fine. My fever was completely gone and my feet were their usual pinkish color. And, yes, I was wearing clean socks. Beck lent me a few pairs of hers. They were coral-reef pink with avocado-green polka dots, but, hey, if they helped keep my feet from being amputated, I'd wear them with pride.

Uncle Timothy saw us packing our gear, getting ready to, once again, traipse through the jungle on our quest for King Solomon's treasure.

"I have to apologize for my outburst yesterday," he said with his hands firmly on his hips.

"In all honesty, kids, I am mightily impressed by what others would surely consider your foolhardy attempts at adventure. Perhaps school will never be the place for children like you."

Uncle Timothy pulled a satellite phone out of his back pocket and pressed a speed-dial number.

"Hello? Chumley Prep? This is Timothy Quinn, legal guardian for Thomas, Stephanie, Bickford, and Rebecca Kidd. My four wards will no longer be attending your fine institution. They will continue on their never-ending hunt for treasure, no

matter the danger, no matter the risk, no matter where that hunt might take them!"

There was a pause.

"Yes, of course I know what time it is." He tilted his wrist so he could read his bulky watch. "Oh-nine-hundred hours."

Another pause.

"Right. Sorry. Forgot about the seven-hour time differential. So I guess it's, what, two AM in New York?"

He held the phone away from his ear so whoever was yelling at him wouldn't puncture his eardrum.

When the screaming stopped, he said to the phone, "Sorry to disturb you. Please relay my message to the headmaster. And good luck with your nocturnal mop duties."

He snapped off the phone.

"That was the night janitor. But, rest assured, he will pass along my message. You four will not be returning to Chumley Prep, and I will move the assets of your trust fund back into the banking account of Kidd Family Treasure Hunters Inc."

Tommy shot out his hand to shake Uncle Timothy's. "Yo, thanks."

I stepped up to shake his hand, too. "Maybe you're not as weird as we all think."

"Thank you for that, Bick. You know, you kids remind me of those other Kidds—your mother and father. No matter the assignment, no matter the obstacles, they were always filled with gritty determination. So go on. Make them proud. Go find King Solomon's Mines. It's what they'd want you to do. But, remember, keep one eye over your shoulder at all times."

We nodded. We knew the Zambian pirates, Guy Dubonnet Merck, and Nathan Collier weren't very far behind us.

In fact, given all the delays our trip down the river rapids and my trench foot had caused, they might be closer than we feared.

Uncle Timothy and Major Lin lifted off in their sleek helicopter.

Over the thrumming rotor wash, we could

hear our uncle who wasn't really our uncle belting out another tune. This time, it was Bob Dylan instead of the Beach Boys.

Judging by the lyrics, it seemed like Uncle Timothy had just heard the local weather report.

CHAPTER 64

That hard rain fell like crazy.

Drops the size of pigeon poop pelted the canopy of tropical foliage, dribbled off leaves, and turned the jungle floor into a muddy lake.

I think this is why they sometimes call jungles rain forests.

The four of us held Dad's yellow rain slicker over our heads like a tarp as we pressed forward through the jungle. The center of the slicker sagged like a bloated water balloon the size of a water buffalo's belly. I stared up at the MADE IN CHINA label and wondered, once again, why Dad had stashed his foul-weather gear in a super-secret compartment on *The Lost*.

ARTIST'S NOTE TO SELF. NEXT TIME, DO NOT USE INDIA INK DURING A MONSOON.

The torrential downpour was of epic, maybe even biblical, proportions.

I saw zebras, giraffes, lions, and elephants pairing off, two by two, looking for somebody to build them an ark. You ever smell a wet monkey? Ten times worse than a wet dog. Trust me.

Through it all, Tommy kept acting more and more like Dad.

And Storm was as steady as Mom.

Beck and I (being Beck and I) still bickered,

but it was much more playful than before I got sick. We had only one Twin Tirade, over the difference between a deluge and a drencher.

But after seven solid days and nights of unrelenting rainfall, we knew we were doomed.

Because our porters and guides—Sonkwe, Lord Fred, and the other guys from the Rent-A-Guide hut—quit.

"Sorry," said Sonkwe, speaking for the group. "It's a union rule. Seven days and seven nights of rain is our absolute limit. We're heading home."

"But," said the chipper Lord Fred, "you lads and lasses are in luck. The pirates who have been assisting Guy Dubonnet Merck are in a similar union, and, therefore, they are also quitting. Monsieur Merck, like you, will be stranded in the jungle, all by himself, what-what?"

"The pirates aren't chasing us anymore?" Tommy said to Sonkwe. "Dude, are you sure?"

"Absolutely," said our (former) lead guide. "The head pirate is my second cousin twice removed. He texted me this morning. Merck is on his own— just like you Kidds."

"Ta, then," said Lord Fred. "Good luck finding King Solomon's Mines."

And just like that, they took off—taking almost everything they'd been carrying with them. We were stranded, with very little food and nothing but Dad's droopy rain poncho for shelter.

Also, there was no one to show us the way forward or the way back.

It looked like the Kidd family had reached the end of its final treasure hunt with nothing to show for it but sopping, wet hair; empty stomachs; and soggy socks.

CHAPTER 65

"**O**kay," said Tommy, about fifteen minutes after our guides and helpers had deserted us. "What would Mom and Dad do in a situation like this?"

"Weep and gnash their teeth a lot?" suggested Beck sarcastically.

"No way," I said. "They'd obviously keep calm and carry on! They'd climb over that whatchama-callit mountain range...."

"The Suliman Berg Mountain Range," said Storm.

"Right! They'd cross those mountains and head into whatchamacallit land."

"Kukuanaland," said Storm.

"Exactly. So that's what we need to do. And we need to make it to Kukuanaland and King Solomon's Mines before Merck does!"

"Quick question, Storm," said Beck. "How come this Kukuanaland isn't on any map? How come Google Earth has never even heard of the place?"

"It doesn't matter," said Tommy. "It *is* on the only map that really matters: Dad's treasure map!"

And so we pressed on, doing our best to pick up our pace.

The rain kept coming down as flood season continued. But we figured if this endless, teeming, steaming nightmare was slowing us down, it had to be slowing Merck down, too.

One night we made a little extra progress in our sleep. The rains were so heavy we slid about a half mile farther down the trail on a slippery mud flume.

It was like tobogganing in our sleeping bags.

The next night, a wide variety of snakes slithered across our faces.

But still, we kept thrashing and machete-chopping our way through the rain-soaked jungle.

We'd wake up before dawn, pack

up everything we still had, and carry it on our backs a few more miles down the soggy, vine-tangled trail toward the looming mountains.

"Remind me how all this is going to help us save Mom and Dad?" Beck said to Storm as we hiked through the kind of muck that could suck your boots off your feet.

"Caesar," Storm huffed in reply. "Thirteen."

"Riiiiight," said Beck.

Neither Beck nor I had any idea what Storm meant. But we slogged on.

We'd do anything if it could help us save Mom and Dad. Even sleep with snakes or ride that mud flume again.

CHAPTER 66

B ut then there was the nightmare-spawning
African rock python.

He'd been hiding on the banks of the next
stream we needed to ford to reach the mountains.
Storm called it the Kalukawe River even though
that particular name wasn't on any map besides
Dad's, either.

At first, I thought the long, floating thing in
the water was some sort of speckled tree trunk.
But then it started to slither and squirm.

Beck screamed first. I was right behind her.

The giant wiggle worm was at least thirty feet
long. No exaggeration. Not even an inch. And it

weighed as much as most linebackers—like, 250 pounds.

If an African rock python coils itself around you, it'll squeeze you and squeeze you until blood spurts out of your eyeballs and every pore in your body. It also has a very stretchy jaw so it can open its mouth wide enough to eat an entire antelope— and most antelopes are bigger than me or Beck.

Plus, African rock pythons eat only meat. No vegetarians are allowed in their snake pits. They chow down on crocodiles, pigs, goats, gazelles, and little children lost in the jungle looking for King Solomon's Mines.

DON'T YOU **DARE** TRY THIS AT HOME

DRAWN FOR THE SAKE OF STORY TELLING ONLY.

30 FEET LONG!

WEIGHT: **250** POUNDS (THE SNAKE, NOT ME)

CAN LIVE FOR A YEAR WITHOUT FOOD IF IT EATS A BIG ENOUGH ANIMAL LIKE, SAY, ME.

Think about all that.

Luckily for us, with the combined might of all four Kidds, we were able to wrestle it out of the water and scare it off before it strangled and ate Beck. (Sorry, Beck, you know you're probably more delicious than I am.)

After our adventure with that snake, I suggest forcefully resisting anyone (like me) who suggests that you go on a treasure hunt to the jungles of Africa.

Next time I'll know better than to listen to myself.

CHAPTER 67

Finally, miraculously, the rain stopped. A brilliant rainbow arched its way to a valley on the far side of what Storm kept calling the Suliman Berg Mountain Range.

"We cut through that pass up ahead," she said, "and we'll be at Sitanda's Kraal."

"What's a kraal?" I asked.

"An Afrikaans word for a circular cattle pen surrounded by a mud wall."

"Is that where the mines are?"

"No. It's just a landmark. Next we'll need to find the sand koppie."

"And what's that?" asked Beck. "A circular horse corral made out of sand?"

"Hardly. It will resemble a giant anthill about a hundred feet high that covers two acres of ground."

"You're making this stuff up."

Storm grinned. "Not me. Come on. We just need to head up Solomon's Road and move closer to the mouth of the treasure cave."

Weary and worn out from our death march through the jungle, we somehow found the energy to run up the trail, through a narrow pass, down into the valley, and—ta-da—right where Storm wanted us to be.

There was only one slight problem. Actually, there were a few.

First, we never saw a cattle kraal or a giant ant mound.

Second, the road we were on didn't have a name. In fact, it wasn't even a road. More like a pair of rutted tire tracks in the mud.

In fact, there was nothing at Storm's mental

"X marks the spot" that was any different from what we'd been seeing for weeks.

"Um," said Tommy, "you sure about this, Storm?"

"Yep. This is exactly where the treasure map will lead."

"Cool," said Tommy. "So, um, where are we?"

"We just crossed the border into the Democratic Republic of the Congo, a country that has been in a constant state of war for years. In fact, the most recent State Department bulletin suggests that US citizens avoid travel to the DRC because of instability and violence."

"So, um," I said, "what exactly are we doing here, then?"

"Waiting for Guy Dubonnet Merck. And maybe Nathan Collier, too."

CHAPTER 68

I f there was *anything* special or different about the patch of jungle where Storm had decided we'd just wait for the bad guys, it was the number and quality of the mosquitoes.

I HAVE **MANY** CLOSE RELATIVES; MANY DEAR FRIENDS; MANY, **MANY** CHILDREN.

NOW MULTIPLY THIS MOSQUITO TIMES ABOUT **5 MILLION**.

There were *trillions* of them.

If you don't believe me, try counting the bites on my legs. You'll hit one million before you reach the back of my knees. Which reminds me: The next time we go treasure hunting in the jungle, I'm definitely packing a pair of long pants.

Some of the aerial-borne bloodsuckers were as big as birds. Some had nozzles the size of turkey basters. And to make the mosquito infestation even worse, Storm kept broadcasting more dismal mosquito factoids.

"Mosquitoes carry malaria, the biggest child killer in Africa. They carry other diseases, too. All in all, mosquitoes are responsible for one million deaths every year, making them the most deadly creatures on earth."

And then, as icing on the jungle cake, while we were losing blood by the pint to mosquitoes, a pack of hostile chimpanzees surrounded our camp.

These weren't happy chimps like you see on postcards and calendars. None of them were wearing business suits or funny hats. None of them were on roller skates. These were angry chimps. The kind that screech, flail their arms, and throw dung balls at you.

"There's at least two dozen of them," said Beck, after taking a quick chimp head count. "They have us surrounded."

"This is bad," I said. "Worse than that movie *Planet of the Apes!*"

"Which one?" asked Tailspin Tommy. "Because they made like a dozen. *Beneath the Planet of the Apes*, *Escape from the Planet of the Apes*, *Conquest of—*"

Yes, Tommy was tailspinning out of control again.

"All of them!" I shouted to jolt him out of his mental nosedive.

The screeching apes tightened their circle around us. They grunted, snarled, flared their teeth, and pant-hooted at us.

We backed up. They moved forward.

How could we possibly hold off an army of angry chimpanzees?

How could we possibly survive?

Those were two very good questions.

The kind of questions people usually take to their graves!

CHAPTER 69

While we were certain we were about to die, guess who was the only one to hatch a plan?

Tommy, of all people. He must have been inspired by all those Planet of the Apes movies he'd seen.

"Get down, you guys," he whispered.

Storm, Beck, and I crouched low.

Tommy hunched over and started stalking around on his hands and knees, making all sorts of "ooh-ooh-ooh" ape noises.

Then Tommy rose up, made himself as tall as he could, put on an angry face, and started pounding his chest with both cupped hands while making tongue-clucking noises that sounded like tumbling coconuts.

The chimps froze.

Tommy beat on his chest again and made more *knock-knock-knock* noises with his mouth.

When he leaped forward, the chimps jumped back.

"Tommy's imitating a silverback gorilla protecting his troop," whispered Storm. "It's something we both saw Dad do once when I accidentally crawled into a lion's cage at the Singapore Zoo."

Tommy roared and thumped his chest again. I was amazed at how wide he could stretch open his jaw. It was almost as impressive as that hippo's mouth.

All the chimpanzees dropped to their knees and bowed their heads before Tommy, their new ape king. The chimp leader started chattering like a total brownnoser.

Another chimp scurried forward and offered Tommy a gift: a sweat-stained French Foreign Legion hat with a battered crown and frayed flap.

It was the same hat Guy Dubonnet Merck was always wearing.

Suddenly there was a rustle in the brush.

The killer chimps hooted and scattered.

And who should come stumbling out of the jungle but a hatless and tattered Guy Dubonnet Merck.

CHAPTER 70

If the jungle trek had been harsh on us, it had been even harsher on Merck.

GREENER THAN RADIOACTIVE SLIME

Merck's shredded clothing made him look like a castaway on a desert island. He'd lost his shoes, and his swollen feet were greener than mine had ever been. His face, arms, legs—every inch of his skin—were riddled with mosquito bites. He hadn't combed his hair or shaved in weeks.

"And so, Kidds," Merck wheezed as he limped forward. "We meet again."

After a prolonged coughing jag, Merck waggled a broken baobab branch at us. It appeared to be his only weapon.

"You four have led me on quite the chase, no? A giant hippopotamus scared off half my men. A crocodile ate all our ammunition." Merck adjusted his mud-spattered eye patch. "An African rock python crushed the last of my food, and, of course, the torrential rains caused my few remaining troops to desert me."

Merck lurched forward another half step and stubbed his toe on a giant African fruit beetle, which snapped at him with its pinchers.

After screaming for maybe thirty straight seconds, Merck continued his little speech.

"But *voilà*! I have finally defeated you, you foolish children!"

Beck and I exchanged a look: *Seriously? He thinks he defeated us?*

"King Solomon's Mines are mine!" Merck, who maybe had a touch of dengue fever, laughed uncontrollably for a few seconds, muttering, "The mines are mine! Mines, mine, mines. Mine, mines, mine."

While he did his drooling happy dance, Storm stepped forward.

"You are right, Monsieur Merck," she said in a stilted voice. "Your street smarts are far superior to our book smarts. The treasure of King Solomon's Mines belongs to you!"

Merck was delirious with joy (and maybe a few snake bites). "*Oui, mes amis!*" And he started giggling that "mines, mine, mines" ditty again.

"Storm?" said Tommy. "After all that we foolish children have been through, here in the jungle"—

Yes, Tommy's acting is a little stiff sometimes, too.

—"you would just give Guy Dubonnet Merck

the sixty trillion dollars' worth of diamonds buried inside the treasure pit barely five miles up the road from where we are standing right now?"

"Yes, Tommy," said Storm. "He wins. We lose. It's time for the Kidd Family Treasure Hunters Inc. business to close up shop."

CHAPTER 71

Okay. As you probably remember, neither Beck nor I was in on Storm and Tommy's big secret plan.

But, judging from their bad acting, and how eager they were to let Guy Dubonnet Merck have all the treasure hidden in King Solomon's Mines, we had to figure that this was all part of some crafty scheme.

"I need a new map!" said Merck. "A chimp swallowed the one I stole out of your hotel room in Cairo!"

"Fine," said Storm. "I'll draw you a new one."

"*Sacre bleu!* You will *draw* it? How?"

"My sister has a photographic memory," said Tommy. "But, before she scribbles a single line, we need to make a deal."

"What sort of deal?" said Merck, hiking up what was left of his pants.

"We give you the map. You let us go."

Merck sniggered. "Of course I will let you go! Go back the way you came. See if you make it out alive."

"You promise you won't come after us with your, uh, stick?"

"I give you my word."

"All right, then. Sis, draw him a map."

And Storm did.

"That path up there, cutting through the jungle, was once known as Solomon's Road. Follow it for about five miles until you see the ruins of the idols. Go down into the pit and you'll see the mouth of the mines."

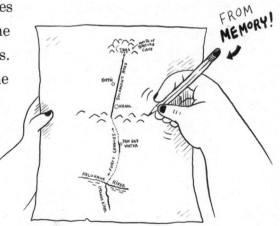

"*Merci*, mademoiselle. *Au revoir*, foolish children! My treasure awaits!"

Merck hobbled up the trail.

At the pace he was traveling, it would probably take him five days to travel the five miles.

"Okay, you two," said Beck, when Merck was finally gone. "Why, exactly, are we letting Merck have our treasure?"

"Because," said Storm, "there is no treasure anywhere near here."

"What?"

"There is no Kukuanaland. No diamond-filled mines."

"But the map…"

"It came out of that paperback novel Dad stashed in the safe-deposit box," said Tommy, pulling out his satellite phone and quickly punching a series of buttons.

"If Merck the Jerk had ever read a book," said Storm, "like, oh, maybe, *King Solomon's Mines* by Sir H. Rider Haggard, he'd know that everything on that treasure map came straight out of a work of fiction."

"Wait a second," I said. "So why did *we* follow the same map? Why'd we risk our lives with trench foot and man-eating crocodiles and mud slides and mosquitoes and crazed chimps if you guys knew the map was a phony?"

"Easy," said Storm. "To prove to Merck that it *wasn't*."

"It's also why we made no secret about where we were headed," said Tommy. "Why Storm kept blabbing, 'We're going to King Solomon's Mines' to everybody we met like it was a trip to Disney World."

STORM's VERSION OF

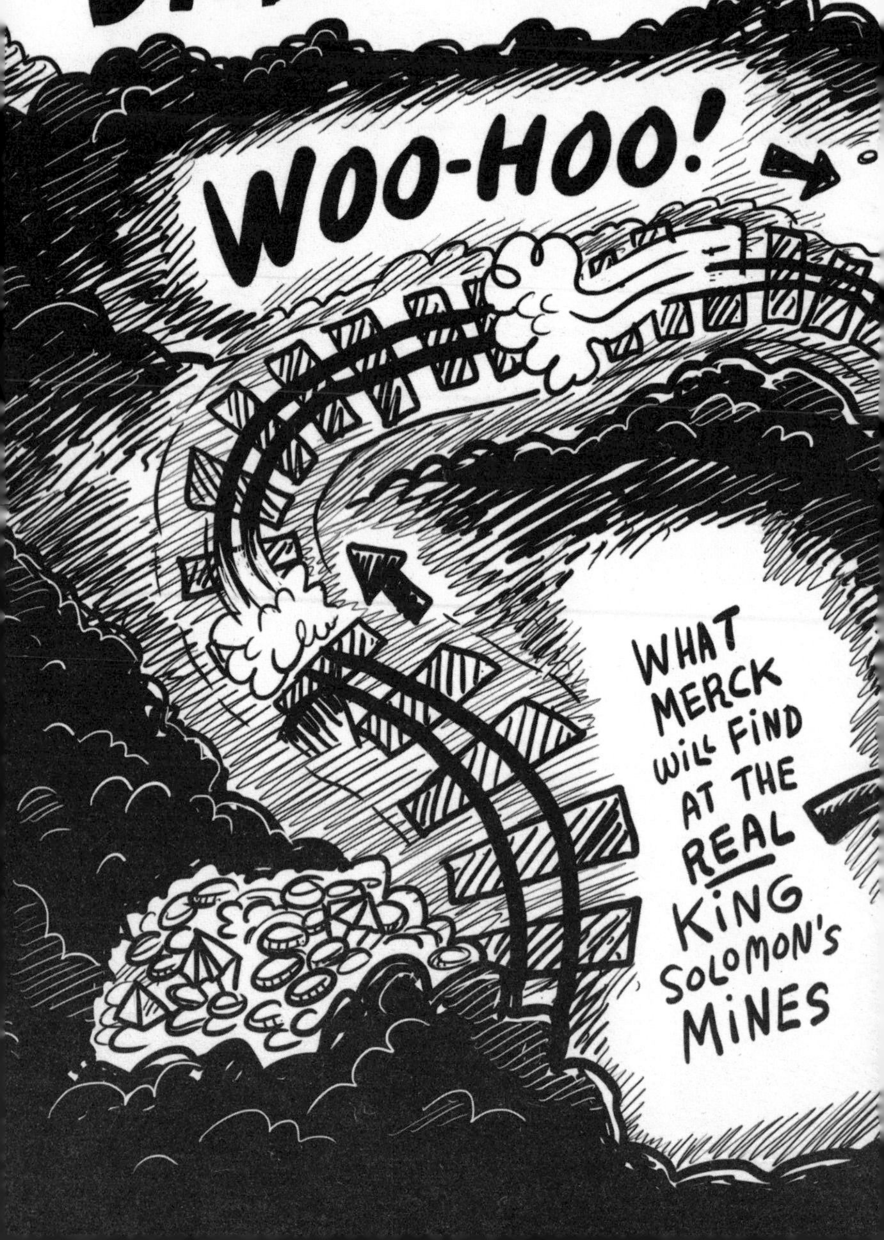

Suddenly we heard the throb of helicopter blades overhead.

"It's our extraction package," said Tommy. "Remember, Dumaka and I set this up back in Cairo?"

The chopper landed in our clearing. Dad's friend Dumaka was in the pilot's seat.

We grabbed our personal gear and loaded up.

"Greetings, Kidd family," Dumaka shouted over the roar of the rotor wash. "Are you ready to say good-bye to the jungle?"

"I was ready a week ago!" shouted Beck.

We lifted off.

The instant we cleared the treetops of the jungle canopy, Storm and Tommy slapped high fives.

"Um, you guys?" I asked. "Where exactly are we going now?"

"The coast of Kenya," replied Tommy. "Now that we're totally and completely rid of Merck, we need to start our *real* treasure hunt! The one that'll set Mom free!"

PART 3

OPERATION: FREE MOM (AND, HOPEFULLY, FIND DAD)

CHAPTER 72

The one-hour helicopter flight out of the jungle back to the village where we had parked our Safari Extreme Global Expedition Vehicle was very enlightening.

Storm and Tommy had finally explained their supersecret plan to Beck and me. We were all hooked up with aviation headsets so we could communicate over the noise of the chopper's thumping blades.

"Remember that slip of paper I found hidden inside Mom's dive watch?" said Storm. "It was a message written in code."

FINALLY, OUR BIG BROTHER AND SISTER TELL US THE TRUTH, THE WHOLE TRUTH, AND NOTHING BUT THE TRUTH!

Working totally from memory, Storm re-created Mom's coded message on a small whiteboard stowed in the helicopter's passenger area:

ZI fzneg naq jbaqreshy puvyqera!
ZI pncgbef urer va Plcehf ner jvyyvat
gb frg zr serr vs lbh oevat gurz n Zvat
Qlanfgl infr gb tb jvgu gur Terpvna hea
gurl npdhverq sebz lbhe svefg nqiragher.
Tb gb jurer lbhe qnq gbyq lbh gb ybbx va
Nsevpn! Ohg or pnershy. Bguref jvyy gel
gb fgbc lbh sebz frggvat zr serr.

"I, of course, immediately recognized it for what it was," Storm continued. "And promptly destroyed the evidence."

"You mean you swallowed it," said Beck.

Storm shrugged. "Whatever."

"Go on," I said. "How'd you crack the code?"

"Easy," said Tommy. "Storm just did what Mom told her to do."

"Huh?"

"Caesar," said Storm. "Thirteen."

"*Oh-kay*," said Beck. "And what exactly is that supposed to mean?"

"Yeah," I added. "That's been bugging me ever since Mom said it."

"Simple," said Storm, because so many extremely complicated things are ridiculously easy for her genius brain to decipher. "In cryptography—"

"That's the study of codes!" said Tommy, who apparently went over all this stuff with Storm back in Cairo.

"Exactly," said Storm. "In cryptography, a Caesar cipher is one of the simplest and most widely known encryption techniques. It's named after Julius Caesar, who used it to keep his private correspondence *private*."

"And what exactly is a 'Caesar cipher'?" asked Beck.

"A substitution code where each letter in the message is replaced by a letter some fixed number of positions down the alphabet."

"Thirteen!" I said.

"So," said Beck, "you knew to substitute every

letter in that jumble with one that was thirteen letters down in the alphabet."

Storm nodded and quickly erased the whiteboard so she could jot down Mom's translated message, reading it aloud to make doubly sure Beck and I understood:

My smart and wonderful children!
My captors here in Cyprus are willing
to set me free if you bring them a Ming
Dynasty vase to go with the Grecian urn
they acquired from your first adventure.
Go to where your dad told you to look in
Africa! But be careful. Others will try to
stop you from setting me free.

Others.

I couldn't help but notice that Mom had used the plural. That meant somebody besides Merck might be trying to stop us from setting her free.

Who could it be? Nathan Collier? Strange Uncle Timothy? Even stranger Aunt Bela Kilgore?

I hated to admit it, but it was probably smart

of Tommy and Storm not to tell Beck and me about this big fake-out. If we had known it was all just a clever ploy to lead the bad guys in the wrong direction, we might not have done such a convincing job faking everybody out. I would have *definitely* bailed when my foot turned green.

Our big brother and sister knew we had to make absolutely, doubly certain that whoever was trying to stop us from setting Mom free 100 percent seriously thought we were slogging our way through the jungle to find King Solomon's Mines—even though that particular treasure never actually existed.

It was just a work of fiction, straight out of a classic book.

Fortunately for us, a lot of bad guys are too dumb to read!

CHAPTER 73

"Woo-hoo!" I shouted into my headset. "Way to go, Storm!"

I slapped her a high five.

Tommy held up his palm. "Don't leave me hanging, bro." So I slapped him five, too.

"Whoa," said Beck. "Hang on a second. Dad told us *four* different places to 'look in Africa.' We've already scratched King Solomon's Mines off the list. But how are we supposed to figure out which one of the other three has this Ming Dynasty vase Mom's kidnappers want so badly?"

"That one's actually easy," said Tommy. "There

was only one treasure map in the safe-deposit box with the word 'Ming' in its title."

"The Ming Dynasty Artifacts from Zheng He's Treasure Fleet," I mumbled.

Tommy reached over and tousled my hair the way Dad used to when I said something smart. "Way to go, bro. You're two for two from the floor."

"The shipwreck off the coast of Kenya," said Beck, getting more excited. "We're going deep-sea diving again?"

"We sure are," said Tommy.

"Speak for yourself," muttered Storm.

"We'll drive the expedition vehicle down to the Lusaka airport," Tommy went on. "In Lusaka, we'll load the truck into a cargo plane that Dumaka arranged for us."

"The transport will fly us up to Nairobi," Tommy continued. "And then—"

Now Tommy's eyes darted around suspiciously, like he half expected Guy Dubonnet Merck or, worse, Nathan Collier to be hiding in the helicopter, listening to everything he said so they could beat us to the real treasure.

"Then we'll drive to the coast," Tommy whispered into his mouthpiece. "To the spot where, you know, we're supposed to go."

Tommy tapped his chest pocket. I'm guessing that was where he had Dad's map to the Chinese treasure ship's wreckage site.

"We'll need a boat," said Beck, shifting into family quartermaster mode. "Scuba gear, salvage

351

equipment, enough food and potable water for a week at least..."

"All of which," said Tommy, "we can buy with the crown jewels of Russia money we deposited in the Kidd Family Treasure Hunters Inc. unofficial Swiss bank account. So rest up, everybody. Once we land at the village and pick up our safari truck, we're going to be very, very busy."

Everybody else eased back into their seats. Storm, Beck, and Tommy were all smiling like we'd already found the sunken Chinese treasure vessel, retrieved a Ming vase, and hauled it up to Cyprus to ransom Mom.

Two seconds later they all had their eyes shut and were grabbing a quick catnap.

Me? I was still worried.

We knew Nathan Collier was lurking somewhere in Africa. Uncle Timothy told us about Collier's submarine docking in the Kenyan port city of Mombasa.

So why hadn't we run into the scuzzy sleazeball yet?

CHAPTER 74

Our freshly washed safari vehicle sat gleaming in the sun outside the thatched hut where we'd stashed it.

Tommy tipped the locals who had guarded our supertruck. Beck and I checked out the cabinets and secret compartments.

"We've got Twinkies!" I announced. "Ding Dongs and Ho Hos, too."

"Excellent," said Beck. "We might need the ammunition if we run into any more pirates on the ride down to Lusaka."

"Do not worry," said Dumaka. "I will be traveling

with you. There will be no more problem with pirates."

The way Dumaka said it, I believed him.

With Tommy at the wheel and Dumaka riding shotgun, we headed for Lusaka.

"So tell me, Kidds," said Dumaka as we rolled down the Great North Road, "where will your journey take you next?"

"Where Mom and Dad need us to go," said Storm.

"I see. And where is that?"

"Sorry," said Storm. "That information is classified."

Dumaka looked sort of hurt. "Really? After all I have done for you and your family?"

"Sorry, dude," said Tommy.

"We have another treasure map," blurted Beck, who, like me, couldn't stand to see the sad expression on Dumaka's face.

"Indeed?" he said. "Might I take a look at this new treasure map?"

"No," we all said at the same time. "Sorry."

"But I might be able to help you navigate the most expeditious route to your final destination."

"I'm really sorry," said Beck. "It's not gonna happen. Just drop it."

Dumaka held up both hands in surrender. "As you wish, children of my good friend Dr. Thomas Kidd. As you wish."

That was when something started buzzing and rattling around inside the truck's center console.

Beck gasped. "Another snake!"

CHAPTER 75

"Relax," Tommy said with a chuckle. "That's just my iPhone. Forgot I stashed it in there to recharge when we took off through the jungle."

Beck opened up the console's lid and jabbed the buzzing phone's speaker button.

"This is Tommy Kidd's iPhone," she said. "Who may I say is calling?"

"Is Tommy there?" gushed a female voice.

"This is Tommy," Tommy said, his eyes fixed on the road.

"Ohmigod! I've been calling you for days."

"Sorry. Been kind of busy. Working on another adventure."

"But where are you?"

"Driving. Um, sorry to ask, but—who is this?"

"What? Don't you recognize my voice? It's me. Gina."

Tommy had a pained look on his face like he was trying to remember which of his many lady friends was named Gina.

She helped out: "The redhead?"

"*Riiiight*," Tommy said very suavely and smoothly. "Gina. How you doin'?"

"Thomas?" said Storm.

"Yeah?"

"Isn't Gina the girl in the bikini who works for Nathan Collier?"

"Nuh-uh," said Gina, who must've heard Storm. "Not anymore. Did you know he styles his hair with car wax? That's why it's always so shiny."

Tommy and Gina chatted some more, until their conversation eventually devolved into kissy-face noises.

I thought I was going to hurl.

Fortunately, Tommy and Girlfriend No. 496 said "buh-bye" (like a hundred times) when we pulled into the Lusaka airport.

"Gotta run," said Tommy, piloting our vehicle up the ramp into another wide-bodied cargo plane.

"Where are you?" asked Gina.

"Um, at the airport."

"Where are you going, Tommy? I miss you."

"Wherever the next treasure map leads. Catch

you later, Gina. And next time you see me, you'll get to meet my mom!"

Okay, that made me smile. If this hunt for an antique Ming vase off the coast of Kenya was successful, pretty soon we'd be bringing home one of the real treasures we were seeking: Mom!

CHAPTER 76

W e said good-bye to our father's friend
Dumaka a few hours later, when we landed
at Nairobi's Jomo Kenyatta International Airport.

"You children are certain you do not wish me to continue with you on this new and possibly dangerous adventure?" he asked when our truck was off-loaded from the cargo transport.

"Yes," Storm said bluntly, once again (not) demonstrating her total command of people skills.

Tommy tried to soften the blow. "Sorry, D. We just, you know, do better when we keep things in the family."

"Of course," said Dumaka. "I understand. Your father always told me, 'family first.' However, because of my, shall we say, 'connections,' I have access to another high-tech helicopter, here in Kenya...."

"We'd rather drive," said Storm.

"Look," Tommy said to Dumaka, "if we change our minds, we'll give you a call. Okay?"

Dumaka nodded. "Very well. I will be spending some time here in Nairobi with my family—my other brother, Joseph. You know how to reach me should your circumstances change?"

"Chyah," said Tommy. "You'll always be speed dial number one on my satellite phone."

They shook hands.

"Until we meet again, Thomas Kidd."

"Later, dude."

We climbed into our suped-up expedition vehicle and drove away from Nairobi into the African bush.

"It's three hundred and seven miles to the Kenyan coast," said Storm, who would act as our GPS navigator for this leg of the journey. "We'll definitely see more wildlife. Our route cuts through the Ngai Ndethya National Reserve."

Which, of course, is exactly the spot (in the middle of nowhere) where we had a flat tire.

And almost lost our lives fixing it.

(Okay, Beck is telling me to skip this part about how we were attacked by wild boars. She says it's just another close encounter of the animal kind and you'll find it very "boaring." Cute, Beck. Cute.)

Of course, what happened *after* we survived yet another wild-animal attack, changed that flat tire, and cruised a little farther down Mombasa Road was even more terrifying.

The number one predator on the entire continent of Africa was lying in wait, blocking our way forward.

That's right.

Nathan Collier had finally found us.

CHAPTER 77

C ollier stood in the middle of the two-lane highway with his hands on his hips.

THE HUMAN BUZZARD.

LIVES OFF THE SCRAPS OTHER TREASURE HUNTERS LEAVE BEHIND.

He was flanked by two goons with Uzi sub-machine guns. Behind them was a NATHAN COLLIER TREASURE EXTRACTORS—emblazoned safari vehicle the size of an eighteen-wheel truck. The tractor-trailer rig was parked sideways across both lanes of the narrow highway.

"Thomas, Thomas, Thomas," said Collier from the road, grinning his toothy smile and shaking his head.

His waxy hair didn't even budge.

"Will you never learn? I warned you once, I'll warn you again: Turn off the GPS chip in your iPhone unless, of course, you want everyone in the world to know exactly where you are at all times."

One of the many side doors on the NCTE truck swung open, and out stepped Gina, the sneaky redhead, wearing yet another bikini.

"Hi, Tommy," she said with a giggle. "How *you* doin'?"

Tommy gripped the steering wheel. Hard.

"I've had better days," I heard him growl as his now ex-girlfriend laughed at him.

Collier stood about twenty feet in front of our bumper. He started marching forward. His two bodyguards racked their weapons and marched with him.

"I'll take the treasure map," he said, holding out his hand.

"We don't have a treasure map!" Beck hollered out a window.

"Except one that'll take you to King Solomon's Mines!" I shouted out my window. "But you better hurry. Guy Dubonnet Merck might beat you to all the diamonds."

"I'm not interested in King Solomon's mythical mines," sneered Collier. "I want the map that you Kidds are currently following. The one that will, somehow, lead you to a priceless Ming vase. As you may recall, children, I have certain friends in Cyprus who tell me *everything* they'd like to add to their rapidly growing art collection."

Yeah, I thought, the scumbags *who kidnapped Mom.*

"And, just a few weeks ago, my Cypriot friends

369

told me that they wanted an antique Chinese vase to go with that Grecian urn you sniveling little brats stole from me!"

"Only after you stole it from us!" shouted Beck.

"Ah-ha! So you *admit* you stole the urn! You four children are nothing but sneaky little thieves. Why, you're no better than the filthy street kids of Cairo who prey upon innocent, unsuspecting tourists."

Tommy had heard enough.

"I liked those kids in Cairo," he muttered. "They told me what cake tasted best at that café."

He jammed his foot down on the gas pedal.

Our hulking truck lurched forward like a hippopotamus.

Tommy was gunning straight for Nathan Collier, who wasn't smiling so much anymore.

His two mercenaries opened fire with their machine guns.

The bullets hit our windshield and bounced off.

"And that," said Tommy through gritted teeth as he swung the steering wheel hard to the right, "is why you should always go with the bulletproof glass option when purchasing an off-road expedition vehicle."

We were tilting up on our tires, burning rubber, heading for the ditch at the edge of the highway.

Tommy jammed forward on the stick, shifting us into all-wheel drive. Our truck righted with a thud as we came out of the screeching turn, and we plowed across the drainage trench and up into the rutted dirt like a rhinoceros that needed to find a bathroom, fast.

THIS IS WHAT TOMMY CALLS DEFENSIVE DRIVING.

After bounding over a few bumpy knolls and scaring a herd of innocent gazelles into a stampede, Tommy swung the wheel hard to the left to put our heaving vehicle back on the paved roadway.

Behind us, I could see Collier and his troops scrambling to board their eighteen-wheeler safari truck, back it up, and turn it around so they could chase after us.

"And this is why Dumaka put in that supercharged engine."

We shot up the road like a cheetah with a rocket strapped on its back. Hey, spend a little time in Africa, and you'll come up with all kinds of animal similes, too.

In a matter of minutes, we had a six-, maybe seven-, mile lead on Collier and his crew.

Unfortunately, that was when something else appeared in our rearview mirror.

Another pickup truck loaded with pirates.

CHAPTER 78

O kay. I'm not an expert on all things piratical, but these pirates looked a whole lot fiercer than the Twinkie lovers who had chased us down a very similar road way back in Zambia.

For one thing, they all seemed to be wearing hooded masks, like the kind medieval executioners used to wear when they chopped off your head with an ax. None of them seemed like they would be interested in prepackaged snack cakes. Plus, to round out the crew, they had *two* guys with rocket-propelled grenade launchers.

"We're pretty close to the coast," said Storm. "Those guys could be Somali pirates. The ruthless kind who hijack oil tankers and cruise ships and kill people."

"You think they'd like to hijack a new truck?" I said.

"What?" said Tommy.

"I have an idea. Slam on the brakes!"

Believe it or not, my big brother did what I told

him to do. He hit the brakes and eased our vehicle over to the side of the road.

"Thomas?" said Storm, sounding slightly panicked. "What are you doing?"

"What Bick told me to do." He turned to me. "What am I doing, Bick?"

"We're going to play 'Let's Make a Deal.'"

"With a bunch of Somali pirates?" sputtered Beck.

"Yep. Pack up your most essential gear, guys. We're dumping this truck. Like, now!"

I jammed Dad's rain slicker and my journal into a small duffel. Tommy stuffed his high-tech satellite phone into one cargo pants pocket and his favorite comb into another. Beck did the same with her art junk. Storm grabbed the book she'd been reading: *How to Win Friends and Influence Pirates.*

Tommy brought the safari truck to a full and complete stop.

The pirates stopped right behind us and, weapons jangling, leaped out of their pickup.

"Don't worry, guys," I said as the pirates swarmed both sides of our vehicle. "If my plan works, we'll kill two birds with one stone."

"And if your plan doesn't work?" demanded Beck.

"I guess there will be four dead birds instead of two: us."

CHAPTER 79

I yanked up on my door handle and, raising both hands high over my head, jumped down to the ground.

"Okay. We surrender! You guys win. Yes, this truck is worth two million dollars, but you can have it."

The one pirate not wearing a mask sauntered forward. His head was wrapped with a more traditional pirate bandana. He wore camouflage fatigues and had an arm draped across a rifle resting casually over his shoulder. He appeared to be the pirate leader.

"Who says we want your truck?" the pirate leader said with a crooked sneer. "Maybe we want you. You four children would fetch a very handsome ransom, yes?"

"Not really," I said, because it was time to spin another lie. "I mean, yes, we would if we weren't orphans with absolutely zero family left in the world to worry about us or pay to get us back."

"What happened to your parents?"

"Dead," I said. "Drowned. You see, sir, our

378

father was a seafaring man, much like you. One dark and dreary night, off the coast of the Cayman Islands, the biggest storm many a sailor had e'er seen blew in from the Bermuda Triangle. Why, the waves were as tall as mountains that night, the winds as fierce as a lion after somebody steps on its tail...."

As I babbled on, one of the hooded pirates went up on tiptoe to peer into the cab of our vehicle.

"Yo," he said. "Is that the new iPhone?"

"Chyah," said Tommy. "*Brand*-new."

TOMMY'S
iPHONE

BLAH BLAH BLAH

BLAH

"We'll take it," said the pirate in the bandana. "And the truck."

"Cool," said Tommy. "Oh, if the name Gina pops up on the caller ID, don't answer it, dudes. She'll talk your ear off." Tommy turned his fingers into yapping puppets. "Blah, blah, blah."

"This Gina, she is your girlfriend?"

Tommy actually winked at the pirate. "One of 'em."

Knowing laughter erupted all around us.

Tommy tossed the pirates the keys. "Enjoy, guys. En-joy."

The pirate leader gave me a two-finger salute off his eyebrow. "A pleasure doing business with you, Mister...?"

"Collier," I said. "Nathan Collier."

"Let us not meet again, Mr. Nathan Collier. If we do..." He sliced his finger across his throat.

"Right. Gotcha."

The pirate leader turned to his comrades. "Board up! We need to be gone from this place! *Maa salama*, Nathan Collier!"

Half the hooting pirates piled into our tweaked-out ride. The others jumped back into their Toyota pickup.

"*Imshy ala tool, thumma 'arrij shimalan*," the leader shouted in Arabic. "We ride for Mombasa!"

CHAPTER 80

The trucks' spinning tires kicked up a cloud of fried rubber and choking dust as the pirates sped off and disappeared over the horizon.

"Brilliant plan, Bickford," said Beck. "We're not dead. We're stranded in the middle of a deserted highway without food, water, or a vehicle, but at least we're not dead. Not yet, anyway. I imagine the vultures won't pick apart our rotting carcasses for, oh, another hour or two."

I was basically ignoring Beck because I was too busy checking out the short, scrubby trees lining both sides of the road.

"This highway won't be deserted for long," I said. "Come on. We need to hide behind that bushy clump over there."

"Why?" said Beck.

"Because Nathan Collier, swimsuit model Gina, and their big rig should come thundering up this road any second now."

"And," said Storm, "with any luck, they'll still be tracking the GPS chip in Tommy's iPhone."

"Which means," said Beck, finally catching on, "they're going to chase those gnarly Somali pirates all the way to Mombasa."

"Unless, of course," I said with a smile, "the pirates see Collier tearing up their butt and pull over to the side of the road like Tommy did."

"Maybe," said Tommy. "But I don't think the Somalis will be in the mood to cut a deal with Mr. Collier. They prefer cutting throats." He made the pirate's slicing gesture across his neck.

"Better if the pirates keep on driving," said Storm. "They're heading for Mombasa. Collier will chase after them. Meanwhile, our treasure map takes us in a completely different direction—north to the Lamu Archipelago."

"Great," said Beck. "And how exactly do you propose we travel to this Lamu Archipelago place without our SUV? Go on another nature hike?"

"Um, I hadn't thought about that part," I admitted.

"I have," said Tommy, pulling out the satellite phone. "As soon as Collier rolls by, we'll give Dumaka a call. See if he still has that second helicopter."

"Wait a minute," said Beck. "If Dumaka gives us a lift, we'll have to show him the treasure map so he knows where to take us."

"True," said Tommy.

"So, all of a sudden, we're going to take a nonfamily member with us to a treasure site?"

"I think we can trust him," said Tommy. "Dad did."

"I don't know....What happened to everything you and Storm were saying in the RV?"

"I'm with Beck," I said. (Yes, twins always stick together. Sometimes.)

"Would you two prefer walking all the way to Lamu?" said Storm. "Did I mention that the archipelago of islands is, like, two hundred miles away? And out in the ocean? It's not perfect, but what else are we going to do?"

Beck and I thought about that for a second.

I also thought about my recent bout with trench foot.

And all the horrible creatures Storm could undoubtedly tell us about that lived between where we were and where we needed to be.

I looked at Beck. She looked at me.

We both sighed and said, "Make the call, Tommy."

At the time, we didn't realize what a huge mistake we were making.

CHAPTER 81

The Collier Express rolled by our hiding place and continued heading southeast to Mombasa.

Tommy called Dumaka on the satellite phone.

Less than an hour later, we were choppering north to the Lamu Archipelago, a cluster of islands in the Indian Ocean just off the northern coast of Kenya.

"Your map makes sense," said Dumaka as he worked the helicopter's joystick. "The island of Lamu is said to be one of the westernmost ports of call for the great Chinese fleet of Zheng He."

Tommy had shared *everything* with Dumaka.

"We also know Zheng He made it to Mombasa in the 1400s," our father's friend continued. "But the legends all say that one of his fleet's gigantic nine-masted ships sank out here, not far from the shores of Lamu island."

"The legends are correct," said Storm, calling up another file in her photographic memory. "In fact, archaeologists have recently proved through DNA testing that survivors of that shipwreck swam to the shores of Lamu island, where they married locals. That's why some of the people living on the island today have Chinese ancestry."

Dumaka put the chopper down at the airport

on a small speck of an island opposite the main village. A ferryboat took us across the water to Lamu town.

Luckily, there were several bank branches in Lamu, so we were able to access the Kidd Family Treasure Hunters Inc. bank account. It was full of cash, so we knew Uncle Timothy had kept his promise. We used some of the funds to rent a fishing boat and reliable scuba gear from a tour operator in Watamu.

We booked three cottages at the Peponi Hotel (our rented fishing boat smelled too fishy to sleep on), where we had dinner on a terrace overlooking the beach and all the dhows—which are those sailing vessels with triangular sails angling off their masts that are so popular in the Red Sea and Indian Ocean. Dinner at the Peponi Hotel was amazing, especially after spending so much time in the jungle eating freeze-dried camping food out of aluminum pouches. I must have gobbled down two dozen giant prawns.

"Breakfast, I am told, is also quite spectacular at this restaurant," said Dumaka.

"Great," said Tommy. "But we better ask for it 'to go.' First thing in the morning, we're heading out there." He pointed to the ocean. "Tomorrow, we're going to find Zheng He's sunken treasure ship so we can grab a Ming vase. Then we're heading up to Cyprus to rescue Mom!"

CHAPTER 82

*A*t first light the five of us (Dumaka was tagging along) stowed our gear and set sail on our rickety fishing boat.

Tommy was in the stern, manning the tiller.

As we followed the chart markings on Dad's treasure map, Storm schooled us on Zheng He and his treasure ships. It's what our mom used to do whenever we were sailing to a new treasure site. The ocean has always been the Kidd family classroom. And treasure hunts? I guess those are our field trips.

"Between 1405 and 1433," Storm said as our boat bounded across the choppy water, "the Ming Dynasty rulers in China sent out enormous armadas of mammoth treasure ships. Each of these gigantic boats had nine masts and four decks, and could carry five hundred passengers plus tons of cargo.

"Zheng He's fleet included three hundred ships, including sixty-two jumbo treasure vessels—each one was four hundred and fifty feet long and nearly

two hundred feet wide. They were the biggest wooden boats ever built, and they explored the Indian Ocean fifty years before the Portuguese 'discovered' it in their dinky three-masted caravels."

"Were they mighty warriors?" asked Dumaka as we reached a cluster of lights and buoys and Tommy made a sharp turn to the east.

"No," Storm said to Dumaka. "Zheng He was out here projecting Chinese pride and power. His voyages were strictly trade missions, even though each treasure ship was equipped with two dozen bronze cannons. They wanted to bring home spices, ivory, rare woods, and pearls from Africa. Plus unicorns."

"Wait, what?" said Beck.

Storm grinned. "Giraffes. When Zheng He presented a couple of giraffes to the Ming royal court in Nanjing," Storm continued, "the emperor's philosophers ID'd the exotic creatures as the fabled *qilin*, or unicorns—even though the giraffes had two horns on their heads instead of just one like a *uni*corn is supposed to."

When we were maybe a dozen miles out of port, a small, jagged landmass appeared on the horizon. Whitecaps and breakers smacked against its rocky sides.

"That's Nubende Rock," said Storm. "That's what the ship we're looking for hit during the pirate attack."

Dumaka shook his head. "This is our destination? I am afraid you, Storm, or perhaps your father, have been given faulty information."

"Excuse me?" said Beck.

"We are too far from the port of Lamu. Many, many miles. There is no way the shipwrecked Chinese sailors could swim all the way from here to safety on the shores of the island."

"Why not?" said Tommy. "We could."

"Definitely," added Beck.

Dumaka chuckled. "I apologize for laughing, children. But what you suggest is impossible. There are sharks in these waters. No grown man, let alone children such as you, could safely swim such a distance."

"Yes, they could," I said. "If their life depended on it and they'd spent their entire lives living on the ocean."

I was remembering how quickly Beck and I had swum across that lake after the hippo dunked us.

"But," said Beck, "your theory probably explains why for over five hundred years, no one else has found the treasure that we're about to bring up from the bottom of the sea. Everyone just figured it was too far away."

Tommy brought the boat to a dead stop.

"Drop anchor, Bick," he cried. "Beck, suit up."

Dumaka looked around at the rippling blue water. "This is it?"

"Yep," said Storm, tapping her map. "X marks the spot."

CHAPTER 83

It was great being underwater on purpose again.

Suited up in our rented scuba gear, Tommy, Beck, and I descended into the murky waters. The only sound was my own regulated breathing. The only light came from the three beacons shining out of our headlamps. Beck and I followed Tommy's trail of bubbles as we dived into the deep waters encircling Nubende Rock.

We were at seventy meters when Tommy put out his flat hand with the palm facing down and

moved it back and forth slowly. It was the command to level off. We were as deep as we needed to be.

As we spread out and Tommy's bubble cloud quit blocking my view, I could finally see the ocean bottom.

And lying there was the shadowy outline of what looked like a toppled, barnacle-covered skyscraper lying sideways in the sand.

It was definitely a Chinese treasure ship!

The claims about its length were true. Below us, I saw the humped carcass of a four-hundred-and-fifty-foot wooden whale.

I could see only four shattered masts jutting through the water. The other five were buried beneath centuries of muck and sand and sea debris.

Now Tommy hand-signaled for us to follow him through a square porthole at the stern of the massive ship that would, hopefully, lead to a lower deck. Carefully, we swam into the Chinese treasure vessel.

With all the cargo compartments, it was like navigating through an underwater maze.

The first small room was filled with casks and barrels and lumpy sacks, which I figured had to have been for holding spices and coffee.

The next room we swam into was extremely tall. We had found the giraffe (I'm sorry, *unicorn*) cabin.

This ship was like a sunken shopping mall, with multiple compartments crammed with merchandise. It would take months to salvage all the treasure on board the jumbo junk. Fortunately, we needed only one piece of pottery.

The Ming vase that would set our mother free!

CHAPTER 84

After swimming through maybe a dozen interconnected rooms, Tommy gave us the "watch me" hand signal. He pulled out his knife and started prying open the nearest wooden crate.

Beck and I followed Tommy's lead. We pulled out our dive knives and set to work ripping open the rotted wooden crates, everyone searching for one thing.

I found spice jars, ivory tusks, and strands of pearls, but no Ming vases.

Tommy scored some broken teapots.

Beck was the first to find what we were looking for: a whole box filled with imperial ceramics glazed in fourteenth-century China, with the markings to prove it.

She held up a cobalt-blue porcelain piece that looked exactly like one Storm had shown us when we Googled Ming vases on the hotel's business center computer.

The Ming vase on the Internet had sold at an auction in Hong Kong for $21.6 million.

Then Beck reached back into the box and pulled out another!

Tommy gave us a big thumbs-up.

When you're scuba diving, a thumbs-up doesn't mean "Woo-hoo! Great job, sis!" It meant it was time for us to head back to the surface.

WOW! A TWENTY-MILLION-DOLLAR FLOWERPOT!

And we definitely had to hurry.

Because while we'd been busy ripping the lids off cargo crates, a giant great white shark had quietly followed us into the belly of the treasure boat.

CHAPTER 85

Panicking, Beck backpedaled as fast as she could.

The giant shark lunged for her flippers.

Beck yanked her legs away from its monstrous jaws a split second before they slammed shut and sent up a massive underwater wake that spun her into a spiral and made her lose her grip on both of the Ming vases.

Our treasures drifted down, twirling slowly, headed for the hard wooden decking below.

Tommy signaled for Beck and me to hightail it

out of that cargo compartment as he dived down to recover Beck's fumble. The shark twisted its torso and thrashed after Tommy, who snagged one vase with his left hand, the other with his right—a half second before $40 million worth of antique Chinese art hit the floor and shattered.

But because of his underwater acrobatics, Tommy was cornered. The shark was circling him, lining up its next attack.

I glanced back into the crates I'd been searching through.

I saw corked jars of...something. I wasn't sure what, but I hoped it was dye. Indigo, maybe. I remembered Mom had taught us about indigo's being a major African export in the days of the spice trade on the high seas.

I grabbed a jar and smashed it against the ship's hull.

Whatever was in the jar wasn't blue, so it couldn't be indigo. It was something better: red and murky. Maybe I had cracked open an antique spice container that had managed to keep its contents safe until I came along. It was red, so it could've been cinnamon? Maybe paprika? Cayenne pepper?

I didn't really care. Whatever it was, it worked.

The shark sensed the swirling cloud of murky redness, and its shark brain bolted to "blood in the water!" faster than a dog's brain leaping to "squirrel!"

EVERY SHARK'S **FAVORITE** SNACK: SPICY-BUFFALO-WING-FLAVORED **BICK**.

Tommy was able to swim out of the suddenly cramped compartment through a side door. Beck had already made it out the way we came in.

That left just me and Bruce and my billowy red cloud of spicy soup.

Yeah, I had already named the monster Bruce after the shark in *Jaws*.

Hey, I figured if a great white wanted to take me out for dinner, I should at least know his name!

CHAPTER 86

Remember how fast I swam across that hippo-infested lake?

Well, I swam even faster through the shark-infested treasure ship. I flew from cargo compartment to cargo compartment like a mouse running through a maze in a mad dash to find a six-pound wheel of cheese.

Bruce stayed with me through every twist and turn.

In that high-ceilinged giraffe cabin, he nipped at my flippers and tasted rubber.

Fortunately, I kept all my toes. But the chewed-up flipper meant I couldn't maintain my optimum speed as I swam into the adjoining chamber—I think it was the rhinoceros room, because there was a pair of petrified rhino skeletons on the floor near a crumbling feeding trough just waiting for me and my puny bones to join them.

I looked up at the rhino room's ceiling, searching for my next exit.

And saw Beck and Tommy waving at me from a cramped passageway.

They were signaling for me to swim up and join them.

So I kicked hard.

Bruce the shark was maybe six feet behind me. His jaws were wide open. From the look of his sharp and jagged teeth, there might not be any bones left for the rhino room's fossil collection after he finished grinding his way through my wet suit.

I found my last extra ounce of oomph and shot through the tiny opening.

I was with Tommy and Beck in a cramped side room. Behind them, I saw a rusty cannon aimed through a porthole. Beck had the two Ming vases in net dive bags securely strapped to her right wrist. Tommy was cradling a cannonball.

Of course, I didn't have much time to enjoy our underwater family reunion on the gun deck

of Zheng He's treasure vessel, because the great white shark shot into the hatchway maybe three seconds after I came out of it.

But Bruce was too enormous to squeeze all the way through the tight opening. Only his toothy snout and icy black eyeballs made it into the gun deck. His thick, gilled neck—not to mention his dorsal and pectoral fins—kept him trapped inside that narrow frame like he was a pit bull wearing a wooden choke collar.

Furious, Bruce thrashed and gnashed his mammoth jaws.

That's when Tommy underhanded his cannon-ball across the room like he was lobbing up a free throw from the foul line. In his fury, Bruce clamped down hard on the lead, probably thinking it was my head.

We didn't stick around to see what happened next. We were too busy flying to the surface like Polaris missiles, but I had a feeling Bruce would probably need to see the shark dentist soon. There's no way he didn't shatter a whole bunch of teeth when he bit into Tommy's rust-flavored jawbreaker.

As we neared the surface, I was feeling pretty good. Make that really good. We really needed only *one* Ming vase to set Mom free, and now we were bringing up two!

I figured we could sell the spare vase at a Hong Kong auction house and score $20 million to throw Mom the biggest welcome home party ever!

Unfortunately, all my party plans had to be tossed overboard the instant we reached the surface.

CHAPTER 87

Ours wasn't the only boat bobbing on the water surrounding the jagged rock outcropping.

Three very sleek military vessels had dropped anchor beside our humble fishing boat. I was pretty sure two were from the People's Republic of China Navy, based on the insignia on their hulls. The other one was probably a CIA ship.

How could I be sure?

Uncle Timothy was standing on the deck. He was surrounded by an entourage of Chinese men with shiny black hair wearing even shinier black suits.

The two Chinese Navy boats were filled with heavily armed men decked out in blue-and-white-striped sailor shirts. They wore brimless admiral hats with bold red stars where the double anchors usually go. Golden Chinese letters were embroidered around the hatbands.

"Well done, Kidds!" Uncle Timothy called to us from the deck of his ship. Then he turned to Dumaka, who was standing next to Storm on the bridge of the rented fishing boat. "And congratulations to you, too, Turkey Trot Two."

I don't have Storm's photographic memory, but I did remember hearing that phrase before: Turkey Trot Two was the person Uncle Timothy had been yammering at in his earpiece when he "miraculously" showed up with trench foot medicine in the jungle.

Dumaka was still a CIA contract worker. Only now, apparently, he was working for Uncle Timothy instead of our dad. No wonder he'd been so eager to travel with us when he learned we had another treasure map besides the phony one for King Solomon's Mines.

Beck ripped her scuba regulator out of her mouth and swam closer so she could whisper to me. "Dumaka knew we were searching for the sunken Chinese treasure ship."

"Because Tommy told him after the Somali pirates stole our truck."

Beck shook her head. "He knew before that."

"What? When?"

"When Storm translated Mom's code on the helicopter flight out of Congo."

"No way. Storm did that on the headsets. Dumaka was busy flying the helicopter."

"And wearing a headset! Remember?"

Yeah. Now I did. *Duh. Pilots always wore headsets.*

I also remembered the Chinese man who had tailed us in New York City, right after we slipped out of Chumley Prep. And Uncle Timothy's Chinese helicopter pilot, Major Lin—not to mention Uncle T.'s newfound familiarity with Mandarin, one of the many Chinese dialects.

"This smells worse than stinky tofu sold on the

streets of Changsha in the Hunan Province!" I whispered.

"What're we going to do, Tommy?" asked Beck.

"We're gonna go along to get along," he said. "And make sure at least one of these Ming vases ends up in Cyprus so it can rescue Mom."

CHAPTER 88

"You have done our nation a great service," Uncle Timothy said as he inspected our treasure haul on the deck of his CIA spy boat.

"Then what's with the Chinese Navy surrounding us?" snapped Beck.

"These Ming vases and the sunken treasure ship down below belong to the people of China, Rebecca. They are of great cultural significance. The Chinese wanted to have proof of Zheng He's voyages to these waters as a matter of national pride. By helping them achieve that goal, we have also helped solidify relationships between two global powers."

"How long have you been searching for the shipwreck?" I asked.

Uncle Timothy grinned. "Ever since your father told me last year that he had a hunch about where one of Zheng He's giant treasure ships might have sunken off the coast of Kenya."

"But you couldn't locate the treasure ship without Dad's treasure map," said Storm.

"It was certainly helpful, wouldn't you children agree?"

"Chyah," said Tommy. "Totally."

"This is why you wanted us in that boarding school!" said Beck. "You had to take us off the game board so you'd have first dibs at finding Dad's map."

"And why you were so relieved when you thought we were actually searching for King Solomon's Mines," I added.

"I admit you kids had me fooled," said Uncle Timothy.

"It was pretty easy," said Storm.

"Speak for yourself," I mumbled, remembering my trench foot and the hippo attack and the giant snake and the mosquitoes and literally *everything* that happened on our horrible hike through the jungles of Africa.

"Was Merck working for you, too?" Beck demanded. "Did you have him 'eliminate' Bela Kilgore so she wouldn't tell us anything about Mom?"

"Merck is an independent contractor," scoffed Uncle Timothy. "A loose cannon. I have absolutely no control over his actions."

Was Uncle Timothy telling us the truth about that or anything else? With those mirrored sunglasses, it's extremely hard to tell, because you can never read the guy's eyes. Either way, the whole thing was devious and disgusting.

But, to tell you the truth, at that moment I didn't really care.

"No matter what," I declared, "we need to send *one* Ming vase to Cyprus! To free Mom!"

"We'll talk to some high-ranking Chinese officials I'm friendly with," said Uncle Timothy. "I'll plead our case. Perhaps they will be willing to let *one* piece go."

"They better," said Tommy. "Because winning Mom's freedom is the whole reason we did everything we did."

When Tommy put it that way, I felt better about my trench foot.

CHAPTER 89

So is Uncle Timothy a good guy or a bad guy? We couldn't decide, and really we still can't.

The next day, we were heading to Beijing, China. Uncle Timothy had agreed to take us along on his trip to present the first of the recovered treasure to highly placed government officials on the Chinese State Council to try to negotiate a deal—one Ming vase in exchange for having done all the work to locate their sunken treasure ship.

Call me an unrealistic, foolhardy, and idiotic optimist (Beck already has), but I was pretty sure everything would work out the way we wanted it to.

Beck wasn't so positive.

But one thing was certain about our trip to China: It was bound to be an adventure!

(Is that really how you want to end this story, Beck? Seriously? Sheesh. How lame is this?)

THIS IS THE PERFECT END ARTISTICALLY. WE FIND THE PRICELESS TREASURE AND ART. WHAT COULD POSSIBLY TOP THAT?
THIS ENDING BITES! THERE'S NO ACTION!!! I'M NOT FEELING A THING!!!
BECAUSE YOU'RE A NUMSKULL WITHOUT FEELING.
AND YOU WENT WITH THE CHEESY SILHOUETTE-SHOT ENDING BECAUSE IT LOOKED PRETTY.
NO, I WROTE "THE END" BECAUSE THE STORY IS OVER.
LIKE I'M OVER YOU!
OKAY, FINE. HOW WOULD YOU END THIS STORY?
I DON'T KNOW. MAYBE BETTER?
THEN DO IT, WRITER BOY.
I NEED PICTURES.
YOU ALSO NEED A BRAIN, BUT YOU NEVER LET THAT HOLD YOU BACK BEFORE.
WILL YOU KEEP DRAWING?
SURE. ONCE YOU START WRITING.

CHAPTER 90

I am happy to report that, since nobody was going to win that particular argument, Beck and I reached a compromise. I can tell you about one more action-packed adventure: the Awesome Boar Attack that occurred when we had to change that flat tire!

I promise you this—the boars were *not* boring! (Whatever, Beck—puns are awesome.)

CHAPTER 91

As I'm sure you remember, we were driving from Nairobi to the Kenyan coast in our souped-up expedition vehicle when, right in the middle of the Ngai Ndethya National Reserve, we had a flat tire.

Tommy and I went out to fix it while Beck and Storm stayed in the truck to continue enjoying the air-conditioning.

Suddenly we heard snorting.

It was a deadly African wild boar.

(Fine, Beck says it was actually a giant warthog. Whatever. It was a huge pig with tusks. Enough said.)

The thing had to weigh two hundred and fifty pounds, and it wasn't cute like Pumbaa in *The Lion King*, either. This beast was ferocious and ridiculously ugly, with all sorts of warty bumps on its head. And the smell? The warthog is a living, breathing, thick-skinned fart.

And it knows how to use those tusks. Fights between males can be pretty violent and extremely bloody. If a warthog senses danger—like maybe it sees a guy holding a tire iron in his hand, about the size and shape of one Bick Kidd—it will attack people. In fact, Tommy told me warthogs will rip off your arms and legs and carry them away to eat, just like a take-home bucket of drumsticks.

There was no time for us to run back into the truck.

The warthog lowered its head and charged.

I did my best to defend us. But I knew Tommy and I were dead meat.

OH, I'M SCARED. I'M TERRIFIED. MY TUSKS ARE SHAKING. IS THAT A TIRE IRON AND A RAIN PONCHO?

CHAPTER 92

A nd then things got worse.

Four more snorting warthogs came charging across the savanna. They'd been hiding in the tall grass and behind the scattered, scruffy trees—just waiting for the word from the head warthog to attack!

It was a full-on, tusk-up charge of the pig brigade.

I fluttered out that yellow rain slicker like a matador's cape, hoping I could trick the pigs into aiming for it instead of us.

But soon the five saber-toothed swine were joined by ten of their closest friends. It was a tusk-bucking stampede swarming across the open grassland aiming for Tommy and me. I couldn't outfox all the warthogs with my matador moves.

What could possibly save us? Because, of course, as you already know, something or someone did save us. But who? What?

Don't forget—this sounder (yes, that's what you call a group of them) of warthogs was angry and hungry, and they weren't backing down!

That's when Tommy and I heard a horrifying, spine-chilling roar.

A pride of lions—at least a dozen—appeared on the horizon.

CHAPTER 93

What would come charging out of the tall grass next? Gustave, that crazed man-eating crocodile? Maybe another bone-crushing African rock python?

"Don't worry!" Storm shouted out a window on the expedition vehicle. "You're saved!"

Easy for her to say. She was inside the truck, not out in the open with no weapons except a tire iron and a yellow rain slicker.

"The lion just happens to be the chief predator of warthogs," Storm continued. For once, I was happy to hear her data dump of fun African facts to know and tell.

"Um, you guys might want to close your eyes," said Beck, who was sharing the window with Storm. "This could get ugly. Like a gross National Geographic clip on YouTube."

Yes, it was "Circle of Life" time.

The lions pounced. The warthogs forgot all about Tommy and me while they ran for their lives (some more successfully than others) and scattered to the four corners of the grassland.

The Kidds (all of us) had lived to hunt treasure for another day!

CHAPTER 94

O kay, so that *was* way more exciting than just ending on a boat bobbing in the middle of the Indian Ocean.

After packing up our treasure and riding the helicopter back to Nairobi, Uncle Timothy bought us—and the pair of Ming vases—first-class tickets on an Ethiopian Airlines flight headed for Beijing.

Yes, the pottery had its own seats. No way was Uncle Timothy stowing those priceless artifacts in the cargo hold.

As we cruised along at thirty thousand feet, the very nice flight attendant offered me a blanket, but I was content to snooze under Dad's yellow rain slicker. It'd been with me every step of the way on this incredible journey. I guess it had sort of become my security blanket. As I tucked the yellow plastic up under my chin, something extremely random suddenly struck me.

I remembered Dad's crude code on the business card for Ronny Venable's Jewel and Soup Emporium that we found in the safe-deposit box back in New York, where he had scratched out a few letters to tell us "always be-ware" when dealing with Venable.

That's when I yanked off my "blanket" and took another look at the label sewn into the raincoat's collar. Remember how I said the slicker was so old that a couple of the letters in the word *made* had been worn down and practically rubbed away?

Maybe they weren't worn down.

Maybe Dad had *scratched* them out on purpose.

Maybe he had been using the same code he'd used on the business card! When I looked down at the label I saw:

Are you reading what I read?
That's right: ME IN CHINA!

CHAPTER 95

I nudged Beck, who was seated next to me. She'd been trying to nap, too.

"What?" she snapped.

I put my finger to my lips.

"What?" she snapped again, a little more quietly.

"Dad is in China!" I said as softly as I could.

"Says who?"

I showed her the tag. "His rain slicker!"

"You're whacked, Bickford Kidd. You know that, right?"

"Maybe. But why else did Dad scratch out the *a* and the *d* in *made* and stuff his foul-weather gear into a secret cubbyhole on *The Lost* in the middle of the worst storm ever?"

"Who said he did all that?"

"Me! I was the last one up on the deck with him. He was wearing this yellow raincoat when he ordered me into the wheelhouse!"

Beck's eyes widened. I could tell she was starting to believe me.

"But why?" she said as we huddled closer so nobody else could hear what we were saying.

"I don't know. Maybe he had to go to China on a supersecret mission. That would also explain why a stealthy helicopter plucked him off *The Lost* in the middle of a tropical storm."

"Okay," said Beck. "What was the mission? What could be so supersecret that Dad would abandon the four of us?"

"He knew we could take care of ourselves," I said.

"True. But what was so important that he'd fake his own death?"

We both thought about that for a few seconds.

And then, in a rare moment of total twin harmony, we hit upon the exact same answer: "Uncle Timothy!"

Now we were both putting our fingers to our lips.

Because Uncle Timothy was only one row in front of us, sitting by a couple of those "high-ranking" Chinese officials.

Beck and I started nodding at each other, because our thoughts were in total sync: Dad had to go undercover inside China to find out what the

I'M DEFINITELY LEANING TOWARD **TOTALLY EVIL** ON THE UNCLE TIMOTHY METER.

CLINK!

heck Uncle Timothy was really up to over there. Uncle Timothy had told us this mission to find the lost Ming Dynasty treasure ship had been done to solidify relations between two global powers: the United States and China.

But what if Uncle Timothy had gone rogue?

What if he was really working for the Chinese?

What if he *had* hired Guy Dubonnet Merck to stop Bela Kilgore from passing on information to us from Mom?

This was why Dad had to sneak into China: to find out if Uncle Timothy was a double agent!

So now we had two reasons to be in China. First, we had to persuade the authorities to give us one of the Ming vases so we could use it to barter for Mom's immediate release. And then we needed to find Dad!

Beck and I were so jazzed neither one of us could go back to sleep.

Because we both realized, after all our adventures in Africa, we were one step closer to finding the *real* treasures—Mom and Dad!

EPILOGUE

CHAPTER 96

You're all invited to come along on our next treasure hunt, in China—and wherever else our continuing quest to find Dad and Mom may lead us!

We guarantee it'll be full of thrills, chills, action, excitement, and fun. Adventures should always be like that. Unless, of course, you die, get seriously maimed, or become a warthog's dinner.

So see you on our next treasure hunt!

Zàijiàn!

(Yes, Beck, that's how you say good-bye in Mandarin.)

IF YOU LOVE THE KIDDS, JUST WAIT TILL YOU MEET THE NEW FAMILY ON THE BLOCK!

**TURN THE PAGE
FOR A SNEAK PEEK AT**

JAMES PATTERSON
AND CHRIS GRABENSTEIN

AVAILABLE NOVEMBER 2014

CHAPTER 1

Hi, I'm Sammy Hayes-Rodriguez. Maybe you've heard of me? I'm the kid everybody's making fun of because my mother made me bring a robot to school with me—the dumbest, most embarrassing thing to ever happen to any kid in the whole history of school. (I'm talking about going back to the Pilgrims and Mayflower Elementary.)

I need to tell you a wild and crazy story about this robot that—I kid you not—thinks it's my brother.

And guess where the dumb-bot got that goofy idea?

From my mother!

Hi, I'm SAMMY'S FRIEND, TRIP. I'M NOT EVEN IN THIS CHAPTER, BUT HERE I AM ANYWAYS.

Oh, guess what? My father is in on this idiotic robot business, too. He even called Mom's lame-o idea "brilliant."

Good thing Maddie is still on my side.

Maddie's absolutely the best little sister anybody could ever have. Aren't her blue eyes incredible? Oh, right. *Duh.* The drawing is in black-and-white. Well, trust me—her eyes are bluer than that Blizzard

Blue crayon in the jumbo sixty-four-color box.

Anyway, Maddie and I talked about Mom's latest screwy scheme over breakfast, which, of course, was served by one of Mom's many wacky inventions: the Breakfastinator.

MADDIE

Punch the button for Cap'n Crunch and cereal tumbles into a bowl, which slides down to the banana slicer, shuffles off to the milk squirter, scoots over to the sugar sprinkler, and zips down to the dispenser window.

THE BREAKFASTINATOR!

Want some OJ with your cereal? Bop the orange button.

But—and this is super important—do NOT push the orange juice and Cap'n Crunch buttons at the same time. Trust me. It's even worse if you push Cap'n Crunch and scrambled eggs.

Maddie and I always have breakfast together before I head off to school. The two of us talk about everything, even though Maddie's two years younger than I am. That means she'd be in the third grade— if she went to school, which she doesn't.

I'll explain later. Promise.

Maddie knows how crazy Mom and Dad can be sometimes. But to be honest, even though she's

WHAT DO YOU WANNA TALK ABOUT THIS MORNING?

ANYTHING. BUT LET'S NOT GIVE AWAY THE WHOLE STORY IN THE FIRST CHAPTER.

younger, Maddie keeps things under control *way* better than I do.

"Everything will be okay, Sammy. Promise."

"But you totally agree that Mom's new idea is ridiculous, right? I could die of embarrassment!"

"I hope not," says Maddie. "I'd miss you. Big-time. And yeah, her plan is a little out there...."

"Maddie, it's so far 'out there' it might as well be on Mars with that robot rover. They could dig up red rocks together!"

Okay, now here's the worst part: My mom told me that this wacko thing she wants me to do is all part of her "most important experiment ever."

Yep. I'm just Mom's poor little guinea pig. She probably put lettuce leaves in my lunch box.

MUST... CATCH... CHEESE!

CHAPTER 2

Mom's "Take a Robot to School Day" idea is so super nutty, she couldn't even say it out loud in front of Genna Zagoren, a girl in my class who has a peanut allergy, which is why my best buddy, Trip, can never eat his lunch at Genna's table. More about Trip later, too. Promise.

Anyhow, it's time to begin Mom's big, *super-important* experiment: me and a walking, talking trash can going to school. Together.

"Just pretend he's your brother" is what my mom says.

"I don't have a brother."

"You do now."

Can you believe this?

I can't.

As for the robot? I don't think he's really going to blend in with the other kids in my class except, maybe, on Halloween.

He's already wearing his costume.

"Good morning, Samuel," E says when we're out the front door and on our way up the block to the bus stop. "Lovely weather for matriculating."

"Huh?"

"To matriculate. To enroll or be enrolled in an institution of learning, especially a college or university."

I duck my head and hope nobody can tell it's me walking beside Robo-nerd.

GREAT.
MOM'S SENDING ME
TO SCHOOL WITH C-3PO.

"We're not going to college," I mumble. "It's just school."

"Excellent. Fabulous. Peachy."

I guess Mom is still working on E's word search program. I can hear all sorts of things whirring as the big bulky thing kind of glides up the sidewalk. The robot chugs his arms back and forth like he's cross-country skiing up the concrete in super-slow motion. Without skis.

I notice that E is lugging an even bigger backpack than I am.

Maybe that's where he keeps his spare batteries.

CHAPTER 3

According to my mother—whose name is Elizabeth—the robot's name, E, stands for *Egghead*, which is what a lot of people call my mom, Professor Elizabeth Hayes, PhD, because she's so super smart (except when she does super-*dumb* stuff like making me take a talking robot to school for anything besides show-and-tell).

My dad, Noah Rodriguez, says the name E stands for *Einstein Jr.* because the robot is such a genius. Ha! Would a genius go to school without wearing underpants? I don't think so.

My sister, Maddie, thinks E is a perfect name all by itself and stands for nothing except *E*.

I kind of like Maddie's idea. Even though Maddie

doesn't go to school, she's so smart it's almost impossible to fight or argue with her about anything. Trust me. I've tried.

But the more time I spend with E, the more I think I know what his name really means: *ERROR!*

"Remember, Samuel," E says when we reach the bus stop, "always wait for the school bus on the sidewalk. Do not stand, run, or play in the street."

A lot of my friends from the neighborhood are already at the corner. Most of them are gawking at the clunky machine with the glowing blue eyeballs that's following behind me like an obedient Saint Bernard.

"What's with the bright blue eyeballs?" I mumble. "Are those like freeze-ray guns?"

"Let's form a straight line, children, away from the street," E chirps. And get this—E can smile. And blink. (But you can hear the mini-motors clicking and purring inside his head when he does.)

"I make these suggestions," E continues, "in an attempt to enhance your school-bus-boarding safety."

Everybody stops gawking at E and starts staring at me.

None of the kids are smiling. Or blinking.

E is definitely the biggest ERROR my mother has ever made—worse than the time she designed a litter-box-cleaning robot that flung clumps of kitty poop all over the house.

"What *is* that thing?" asks Jackson Rehder, one of the kids who ride the bus with me every morning.

"Another one of my mother's ridiculous robots," I say, giving E the stink eye.

"What's his name?"

"E. For *Error*. Just like in baseball."

"I'm sorry, Samuel," says E. "You are mistaken. You are imparting incorrect information. Your statement is fallacious."

Great. Now the stupid robot wants to argue with me? Unbelievable.

Stick around. This should be fun.